THE VENI(

A fantasy
set in the mag
of today and tin... gone by

by Ermanno Libenzi

Contacts
ermannolibenzi.wordpress.com

Cover design: Alexander Powell

Summary

The Venice Tales. An outline
Page 4

Chapter one
Page 7

Chapter two
Page 17

Chapter three
Page 22

Chapter four
Page 27

Chapter five
Page 34

Chapter six
Page 39

Chapter seven
Page 46

Chapter eight
Page 62

Chapter nine
Page 73

Chapter ten
Page 80

Chapter eleven
Page 87

Chapter twelve
Page 100

Chapter thirteen
Page 112

Chapter fourteen
Page 120

Chapter fifteen
Page 139

Chapter sixteen
Page 147

Chapter seventeen
Page 154

Chapter eighteen
Page 163

Chapter nineteen
Page 176

Chapter twenty
Page 185

Chapter twenty-one
Page 196

The Venice Tales
An outline

The Venice Tales is an unusual fantasy novel brimming with characters, places and historical periods. Its narration follows several different plots, all running together towards the end of the story in a whirlwind of fun.

This story has the obvious purpose of amusing its readers, yet its present-day characters, as well as its historical and mythological ones, also provide an opportunity for understanding the spirit of the city, and learning about the millenary history of the Republic of Venice, its great sailors, explorers and merchant-adventurers, its famous, world-renowned artists and architects.

So, through this book, young readers will better understand the heroic accomplishments of the courageous people who built their city in the water and mud of a lagoon, and despite this, succeeded in making an absolute masterwork out of an impossible task.

The story begins with the arrival in Venice, as tourists, of an aristocratic English family, Lady Matilda, Lord Edward, their daughter Gea , and their dog, Alvin, a high-spirited fox-terrier. Unknown to anyone, Gea and Alvin are magically able to talk to each other.

The little dog is the one who sets the whole story in motion. Everything stem from the fact that Alvin meets a group of wandering mongrels, dirty but free and sprightly, in a little square of Venice. Suddenly he hears the call of the wild, and decides to run away with them.

With Alvin's flight, the peaceful holiday of Gea and her parents turns into a wild, and often fun, hunt of the fugitive. The chase along Venice's maze of lanes, up and down its four hundred bridges, will lead them to discover the enchanting beauty of the city.

Many other characters will gradually be introduced to the reader. Among them, three international thieves, Neptune, god of the sea, Bartolomeo Colleoni, the Captain General of the Venetian army, a carrier pigeon, a dolphin and other animals and statues, all talking magically. Their lives and stories will mingle in a dizzying merry-go-round of events. At the end of the book, all the characters will come together in St Mark's square, concluding the story in a grand finale.

Ermanno Libenzi is a writer and journalist, and was born in Milan, Italy. He has written more than thirty books of various genres: tales, novels, science fiction, adventure stories, short stories. Many of his books have been translated in various countries all over the world, mainly in the United States, United Kingdom, France, Germany, Spain, Japan and China.

Recently, he also published on Amazon the new edition of one of his most successful books, "The Planet of Nuts", initially printed in Italy, France and Japan. It is an ecological science-fiction story, a satirical picture of our super-high-tech future. An unaccustomed book apparently looking back to the past with nostalgia, but its true message is another: technology is not an end in itself, progress is really progress only if it doesn't run so fast and wild as to forget common people and leave them behind.

Other successful books of this author are "Robin and the Pirates", "Ernest in the Wild West" and "The Adventures of Ernest in Africa". As the titles suggest, they are adventure stories, wonderfully illustrated, tailor-made to children of all ages and also appreciated by an adult audience.

"A thing of beauty is a joy for ever"
(John Keats)

Chapter one

Phoebus was swooping along high up in the September sky - a delicate, gentle sky, slightly misty with the recent heat of Summer. He had been flying without rest for nearly ten hours, but now he was still beating his wings strongly in a tireless rhythm.

Phoebus was a carrier-pigeon.

On his left leg he carried a small aluminium holder which had a message in it.

He was wondering how much more sky he had to cross before he reached his destination. Lowering his head, he ran his eyes over the space beneath him. Again and again, he took in the swept of horizon, but he couldn't recognize any of the places he was flying over.

No doubt the wind had blown him off course without his realizing it.

He was just going to change direction - to get back on the right course - when, from the thin strip of sea that in the fair distance separated the sky from the earth, he saw a vague glittering, a flickering of golden light.

For a moment, Phoebus was seized by uncertainty, wavering between his duty, which insisted he should get back on his usual course, and his curiosity, which drew him towards the sea, towards the strange light he had seen on its surface.

"After all, there's no harm done if I arrive a bit late," he finally told himself. "I've got a right to enjoy myself now and then, just like everybody else!"

He turned his tail feathers, banked to the right, and plunged forward decisively to his new destination.

As he flew nearer to it, it seemed to glitter more and more brightly. He let his body swoop down gently in the air, and the smooth turquoise of the sea seemed to float up towards him.

Little by little, as the light mist thinned out and eventually disappeared, Phoebus got a clearer and clearer view of the place he was heading for.

"But… it's a city!" he exclaimed. "A city in the middle of the sea!"

Wondering how such a thing was possible, he quickened his flight, impatient to understand the mystery of this city he had never seen before.

A dazzling white light rose from its marble and stone. Here and there the sun set rainbow-coloured reflections trembling on its windows, its smooth weather-beaten marble, the gold in its mosaics and statues.

And the city streets were of water!

The sea not only surrounded the city on all sides, but penetrated it, and ran between its houses, criss-crossing it with a thousand blue veins. The largest of these canals was S-shaped and crossed the city, dividing it in two.

"Perhaps it's a floating city," murmured Phoebus, coming down in wide circles. "Or maybe it's a dead city, half-submerged by the sea…"

But he soon realized there was plenty of life in the city. Its canals were plied in every direction by launches, rowing boats and motor boats. Flights of seagulls moved in white flecks and dots across the panorama. In the squares, along the sides of the canals, and over the countless bridges, there moved a lively and coloured mass of people.

Below him Phoebus could see, churches with high bell towers, marble palaces with façades built as delicately as lace, triumphant domes, spires, diadems, and pinnacles.

On the roof of the houses there was a forest of odd-looking chimneys of every size and shape; on the most beautiful buildings there stood a crowd of marble statues, that seemed by a miracle to be hovering in the air - saints, knights, madonnas, prophets, archangels, emperors, scholars, adventurers...

Phoebus saw a great square spread out beneath him. There was a fabulous basilica that the sunlight turned into a blaze of gold. In front of it, the highest of all the bell towers of the city. Beside the basilica, an immense pink and white palace, as old and powerful as a castle yet as light as if built of sea-foam. All around, a spectacular parade of palaces adorned with a multitude of statues.

In the square, scattered amidst a huge crowd, hundreds and hundreds of pigeons were milling around.

Phoebus came down and perched on the stone shoulder of an angel. He took a deep breath and turned to another pigeon, who was dozing on the statue's right hand.

"Eh, friend, tell me something," he said. "What in heaven's name is this strange city?"

"Why strange?" the other pigeon replied. "I don't know what you mean."

"Well, strange because it's in the middle of the sea, and its streets are water. Have you ever seen any other city?" asked Phoebus.

"No, I haven't."

"They're quite different, you know. But anyway, what's this city called?"

"Venice," the pigeon answered. "Have you come very far?"

"This morning I was five hundred miles away," said Phoebus. "I'm a carrier-pigeon."

Down below, groups of tourist were having their photos taken amongst the pigeons, who were being given generous handfuls of grain at each photo.

9

"A nice life you lead here," remarked Phoebus, whose wings were aching after his long flight.

"Why don't you stay then, there's place for everybody," the pigeon pointed out. "This angel's left hand, for example, is free. As you can see, my place is on the right one."

"I'd like to, but I can't. I'm on a mission."

"You mean you're leaving at once?"

"Yes, I must, unfortunately," Phoebus replied sadly.

"Without even meeting the Lion?"

"What Lion?"

"The Lion of St Mark's, of course, the symbol of the city. He knows lots of marvellous stories. Shall I take you to see him?"

"Well, I... really..." Phoebus stuttered in embarrassment.

"Oh, don't be afraid. The Lion isn't dangerous. Look down here..."

Phoebus looked in the same direction as the pigeon, and there, on the top of an enormous column standing at the side of the square, he saw a majestic bronze Lion with huge wings. On its back, its wings, its tails and even on its head, there were perched countless birds.

"As you can see," the pigeon said to Phoebus, "we're good friends with the Lion."

They took off from the angel, and after a brief flight, came to rest on the top of the column, right under the Lion's muzzle. Phoebus' friend poked his beak upwards and tried to attract the statue's attention.

"Mr Lion," he said, "I've brought a stranger here. A carrier-pigeon who'd like to meet you and hear some of your stories."

The Lion looked at the newcomer, then addressed him in a deep mysterious voice.

"Welcome to Venice, traveller," he said. "Today, to tell the truth, I'm rather tired. I've already told my stories to a Greek seagull, a family of French swallows and even a parrot who'd escaped from a Brazilian ship." The Lion stopped a moment, cleared his throat, and then went on. "At this time of the year there are lots of tourists about and at my age you easily get tired. Unfortunately my 1500 years are beginning to tell on me…"

"Oh, come on Mr Lion," begged Phoebus' friend. "This visitor has to leave soon. Just tell him something about the columns and your trip to Paris…"

The pigeons standing on the pedestal did not ever wait for the Lion's answer. Cooing happily they spread out fanwise in front of him, ready to listen, perhaps for the hundredth time, to one of his tales.

"All right, then, I give in," the Lion said resignedly, and let out such a deep sight that it ruffled all his listeners' feathers. "First I must tell you then," he began, addressing Phoebus, "that, for centuries and centuries, Venice was the capital of a splendid and very rich Republic. Venice had little territory but, all the same, she was powerful because she dominated the seas. Her war galleys, her squadrons of galleons, and her great merchant-vessels carried her name far and wide, from the coast of Africa to Persia, from Constantinople to the heart of Asia.

For more than seven hundred years the Venetians navigators and explorers voyaged to all the coasts of the known world. Giovanni Caboto, and his son Sebastiano were the first, in 1497, to reach and explore the Canadian coasts. The most famous of these Venetian merchants and explorers was Marco Polo, who, travelling through several European and Asian countries, eight hundred years ago reached China, where he met the emperor Kublai Khan.

11

Venetian merchants unloaded the Republic's goods - wood, cloths and handcrafted metals. In return they loaded their vessels with silk, precious stones, gold and silver, dyestuffs, grain, wine, sugar, and spices."

"What were *spices*?" asked Phoebus.

"They were precious substances used for flavouring and preserving food," the Lion replied, "and also for making perfumes. Some of the most sought-after spices were pepper, ginger, cinnamon, saffron, and nutmeg. Beside spices and the other goods I've mentioned, the Venetians were clever merchants, and always tried to buy, or to exchange with their goods, anything beautiful they came across during their voyages. And thus, if I may say so, together with many other treasures and works of art, Venetian merchants loaded me onto a galley, brought me back to Venice and then, at the end of their voyage, they unloaded me on the quay just over here."

As he said this, the Lion pointed out the nearby quay of white stone, against which a flurry of small waves were continually breaking. "But now I want to tell you how I came to be up here. Do you see the column I'm standing on?" he asked Phoebus.

The pigeon leaned over the side of the pedestal and watched the tourist who were strolling round the square. From such a height the tourists' head looked as small as grains of maize. The pedestal the birds were perched on stood, as the Lion had said, on the top of a huge column of grey granite.

"Do you see that other column down there?" the Lion asked again.

Phoebus looked at the column the Lion was pointing to. It was quite near and was made of pink granite. On top of it St Theodore stood on the back of a great crocodile of white stone. The saint was stubbing the crocodile with a long spear.

"About a thousand year ago," the Lion went on, taking up his history, "these two columns, together with another, a third one, were brought to Venice from far away Constantinople. In those days there weren't machines like the modern ones to help you transport things, and the ship were much smaller and lighter than the steel giants I see sailing past every day. So to load the columns onto ships, hundreds of men had to work hard and long on great scaffold built on tree-trunks. Very very slowly they hauled the columns onto the scaffold with strong ropes and then lowered them gently and painstakingly onto the decks of the galleys. Eventually the galleys reached Venice, and with the same system, work was begun on unloading the columns. Two columns were lowered onto the square without a hitch, but while they were unloading the third, the scaffolding and the ropes gave way under the immense weight. With a tremendous splash the column plunged into the sea, causing a wave that swept some workmen off their feet and almost sank the nearby ships. The column is still lying there on the sea-bottom, only a few yards away from the tourists strolling along the quay."

The Lion stopped talking and with a patient look at his tiny listeners, said: "Look, my friends, what do you say if we go on tomorrow? Today I'm tired, I told you before…"

"We want to hear the end of the story about the columns!" some of the pigeons cried.

"And the story of your trip to Paris!" Phoebus' friend added.

The Lion smiled and glanced up at the sky in mock despair. "All right, all right," he said, "just as you like. I suppose I can manage after all. Well, then… the two columns were dragged a few yards into the square. And there, in all their massive bulk, they lay for years and years. There was nobody, in Venice or nowhere else, who knew to lift them and set them upright. For the boys who used to play around the columns from morning to night, every unsuccessful attempt to raise them up was a treat. For them, the best moment was always when the workmen packed up their robes and their strange and useless instruments, dismantled the scaffolding and went off. A minute later, all the boys were once again leaping on the columns or sitting astride them.

But this didn't go on for ever. One day - a black day for the boys - an architect named Nicola Staratonio came to the square. He measured the columns in all possible ways, made some mysterious calculations, and then, with a great team of workmen, set to work. They tied the columns up like large sausages, built an ingenious kind of scaffolding round them, and, with great skill and effort, raised them upright. They fixed them exactly where they stand today. It was 1172. The Doge, that is the Prince of Venice, wanted to reward Nicola and so he gave him the right to set up a stall for games of chance at the front of the columns. Thanks to his concession, Nicola soon became a rich man.

As for me, they put me here some time later, and here I stayed until 1797, when Venice was occupied by the French. Just listen to what happened to me then. One day, the leader of the French, a little man called Napoleon, came and strolled round my column, looking up at me from all angles, craning his neck to see better. Then he pointed up at me and said something to the officers who were with him. Next day they pulled me down, loaded me on a ship, and after a long trip by sea and land, I reached Paris.

They say Paris is a beautiful city and no doubt it is, but not for me I assure you, I didn't like it at all. I'd been in Venice too many centuries to get used to a new city, without counting the fact that there's no sea in Paris… Well, to cut a long story short, eighteen years later they brought me back to Venice and put me on my dear column again, and since then I've never left it."

When he had finished, the Lion raised his head and looked into the distance, standing stock-still in a solemn pose.

He would speak no more that day, the pigeons understood. They said goodbye to him and took flight, spreading out in the clear sky over Venice.

Phoebus and his friend went back to the angel's hands.

"What I like about the Lion," said his friend, "is the way he's simple and modest. Anybody else in this place would be proud and look down on everybody, which, come to think of it, would be easy enough from his position. He's always been the symbol of the loveliest city in the world. For centuries and centuries his figure has been embroidered and painted on thousands of flags and coats-of-arms, he's been printed on coins, and carved on the monuments and the façades of palaces in all the towns conquered by the Venetians. And yet, as you saw, the Lion doesn't boast about it. It's a fine thing, isn't it?"

"Yes, very fine," replied Phoebus deep in thought. He had suddenly remembered his mission and this had made him sad.

Perhaps understanding what had come over him, his friend asked: "Well, are you really sure you want to leave?"

"I don't know," Phoebus replied. "I ought to."

"The Lion knows marvellous stories. The ones you heard today were only the beginning. And after all, who says you have to go?"

Phoebus was silent for a few minutes. "In fact, there's nothing urgent in this message," he said. "Those people do it just as a pastime." He suddenly took the little holder with the message in it off his leg. "They could send a letter. Or they could phone, if they're really in a hurry."

A flock of pigeons rose from the square, fanning out in the sky. Phoebus and friend darted into the air and joined the others. Beyond the palaces, the sea rose and fell gently, like the breast of a sleeping giant.

Chapter two

With a subdued breath of air, the Rolls Royce slid through the green silence of the countryside. At the wheel was Lord Edward Peacock himself, an English nobleman. Next to him sat his wife, Lady Matilda, and sprawling luxuriously on the back seat, there was a thirteen years old girl, their daughter Gea, and Alvin, a black, brown and white fox terrier.

Gea leaned forward to look at the road.

"Dad, is it far to Venice now?" she asked.

"I don't think so," the man replied. "A few more miles and we'll be there. Are you tired?"

"No, I'm just keen to see what it's like, that's all."

Gea turned and settled herself comfortably. And just to pass the time, started teasing Alvin.

"Grunf," protested the dog, who wanted to sleep.

Lady Matilda turned round looking worried. "Alvin must be hungry", she said, and added, stretching her arms out for the dog: "Can you give him to me, please, Gea?"

It was thus that Alvin, waking up, found he had a large chocolate in his mouth, and this was followed immediately by three vanilla biscuits one after the other. He didn't even try to protest: his mistress would have misunderstood and gone on feeding him.

"Poor dear, poor Alvin, so tired," crooned Lady Matilda, cuddling him. "Just look how pale he his..."

"Matilda, for heaven's sake," her husband begged. "Since we started this trip, Alvin's done nothing but sleep."

"Of course, that just shows how tired he is," insisted his wife. "Oh, his coat's all ruffled up, now..."

Before Alvin could move to defend himself, she had taken a small comb out of the compartment near the dashboard and started combing down his fur.

Patiently, Alvin watched the meadows and the trees passing by outside the window. A little later, as soon as he sensed that the combing operation was over, he closed his eyes. In fact, as disgusting as a wet shoe, as inevitable as autumn rain, he felt and smelt the usual spray of lady's perfume falling over and around him. That perfume drove him crazy both because he disliked perfumes in general, and specially the lady's ones.

The black Rolls Royce entered a small town, left it behind, and suddenly the lagoon appeared. Now, its headlights goggling with surprise at the view, the car was speeding across a very long bridge.

To the left and right there lay water that was as smooth as silk, and across it there snorted large cargo-boats. Groups of seagulls were perched on the thin strips of land that stood just above the level of the water and on the thick poles that had been driven into the sea-bed. Some of the gulls were skimming the water's surface, now and then uttering their shrieks of piercing laughter.

"Venice, built two and a half miles from dry land, until 1931 was a real island, which could only be reached by sea." Gea red from the travel-book. "That year Venice was joined to the dry land by a bridge that rests on 228 arches."

"It's the one we're crossing now, I imagine," said Lord Peacock.

Gea thrust the book aside and putting a hand on her mother's shoulder, stared ahead. In the distance, where the bridge ended, the horizon was broken by the jigsaw outline of roofs, domes and bell towers.

"Here's Venice!" the girl cried, stretching out an arm. "Here we are at last!" She took the dog, lifted him up and showed him the road. "Look Alvin, you look too!"

Alvin looked, but except for the seagulls, which caught his attention immediately, the view hardly interested him at all.

The last few miles of asphalt slid past quickly, and soon, at the end of the bridge, they came to a large garage.

The Rolls Royce, which for the last few minutes had been keeping her headlights wide open for a good look at the unusual place they were heading for, unexpectedly found herself turning right, and before she could say Jack Robinson, was moving in the half-dark inside the garage.

She went up a spiral ramp, one floor, two floors, three, and then the last, where she was stopped beside a large window. Outside, in an unbroken sequence, there glowed the unreal scene of Venice.

The passengers got out, took their luggage, and went away.

At first, the Rolls Royce, who had fallen under the spell of the panorama, did not realize she had been abandoned. When she came to, her masters were already far away.

"Ungrateful wretches, traitors!" she muttered, angrily rolling the bulbs of her headlights. "Playing a trick like that on a lady, treating me worse than a milk truck! Why should they leave me outside the city, I'd like to know! We were together in Paris, Rome, Berlin, Madrid, Lisbon, Prague... everywhere in fact! So why not here?"

A chorus of sighs rose from the other cars in the garage.

"What about me then?" moaned a large Cadillac. "I made the trip from America to Europe closed inside the belly of a ship. And only a couple of days after getting out of it, they stuck me in here. If this is Europe, I'd say it's a pretty gloomy place..."

"I won't put up with such an insult!" the Rolls Royce started again. "I'll get my own back, at the first opportunity I'll break down and leave them stranded on the road, even if means losing my reputation!"

"Nobody's worse off than me!" put in a Swedish car. "For eight months of the year I live in the freezing cold: imagine how happy I was when I heard my masters were bringing me to Venice! «At least you'll get some sunshine, my dear,» I said to myself. «It'll do your joints good.» But they pulled a fast one on me: I've been shut up in here for nearly a month!"

A small Italian white car, a Fiat, that had kept silent till then, joined the discussion. "Don't get angry, friends, there's no reason to," she said calmly and persuasively, like someone long used to consoling her neighbours.

The other cars, frowning, turned to her. They looked her up and down, but when they saw she had a Venice number-plate, they calmed down and were ready to listen.

"I used to lose my temper like you at first," the Venetian car said. "Then, one day, I was standing by chance on a landing-stage near here and a motorboat moored there told me the facts of the matter. Cars, my dears, cannot enter Venice."

"Can't enter Venice?" a hundred astonished voices echoed in the half-dark.

"Is there a law against it?" a German Mercedes demanded indignantly.

"No," the Venetian car replied. "It's simply that cars can't go there because the roads are made of water."

"Well, that's a good one," a French Citroen commented. "How do the people get about then? Walking on water?"

"By the *vaporetto*, which is a kind of water-bus, by large motorboats, by launches, or by *gondolas*, the typical Venice boats, " the Venetian car explained. "Otherwise, if they want to walk, they use the lanes and have to cross a lot of bridges. There are four hundred of them, in Venice."

"Ha ha! I bet they enjoy *that*," sniggered a Ford. "They'll miss our nice, comfortable seats in a city like this…"

"Oh dear, I'm afraid that's not true," sighed the little Fiat. "I've been here a long time, and you can't imagine how many tourists I've seen coming back to their cars after visiting Venice. Do you know what they usually say?"

"Er … ahem… no, tell us," the Rolls Royce replied in a voice that was meant to sound indifferent but was trembling with emotion.

"They say: «Ugh, what a terrible bore all these cars are! We've been better off without them!» Or they say: «Walking really keeps you fit, and in Venice you're forced to walk. Instead, with a car…» But that's not all. I've heard a lot of them say: «Wasn't it marvellous, walking without a care in the world, safely, right in the middle of the street?» And others would answer: «You're quite right there: if there aren't any cars, it's quiet and the air's clean and fresh.» Have you got it? That's what our masters think of us!"

"After all the toil and trouble we've been through for them," sobbed a Volkswagen.

"How humiliating…" sobbed a Jaguar.

Two big tears slid from the Rolls Royce's headlights, glistened for an instant on the silvery bumpers and dropped silently to the ground.

Chapter three

After leaving their car in the large garage, Lord Peacock, his wife and his daughter Gea had their luggage carried to the nearby quay, where it was handed over to the motorboat of the Grand Hotel. Lord Peacock, in fact, had booked a suite there.

"Have the luggage put in our rooms," he told the motorboat driver, "and say we'll be arriving later in the afternoon." Then, turning to his wife and his daughter, he added: "And now, my dears, we've come to the beginning of our adventure in Venice!"

After walking only a little way into the city, they could already feel its magic working on them, its colours, sounds, sights and smells: different sensations yet all blended together and producing a single emotion.

The colours of the houses, the shadows of the bridges, and the light of the sky, seemed to lie gently on the canals' dark green water as if on a delicate mirror. As the boats and launches passed, their wakes spread out in countless ripples arching their backs and dancing their capricious way towards the walls of the palaces. You could hear the quite voices of the passers-by, their muffled footsteps, the lapping of the water against the moss at the foot of the houses, and, from time to time, swallows twittering in the distance. And everything was enveloped in the smell of salt water and ancient stone.

Our friends went into the labyrinth of little lanes choosing their way at random. The further they penetrated, the more beautiful and mysterious the city became.

They were so fascinated by it that, for the first time in any of their trips, Lord Peacock forgot he had his camera slung around his neck. So as to move more freely, Gea had taken the dog's lead off his collar, and Alvin, realizing he was in a very unusual place, had started frisking about happily, peeping out from the tops of the bridges, slipping through the people's leg, poking his nose in the shop doors, and barking at the passing boats.

Eventually they came to a little square.

In one corner of the square, in front of a small palace, the white tables of a restaurant could be seen lined up along the pavement. They came closer and saw, through the restaurant window, a gorgeous display of gleaming pink fish, sides of ham, lobster rampant, peaches and black bottles of wine.

They suddenly realized they were hungry, and sat down at a table. They ordered a tasty meal cooked in the Venetian way and accompanied by a good wine, rice and peas, and liver with onions. An ice-cream with peaches ended their order.

The waiter was just going away when he was stopped by a sudden shriek. It was Lady Matilda.

"Alvin! We've forgotten Alvin!"

Alarmed, Gea and his father looked under the table.

"No, no, my dear," the man said soothingly. "Alvin's under there."

"I know he's under there," replied Lady Matilda. "I mean we've forgotten to order lunch for him."

Lord Peacock turned to the waiter. "And a bowl of rice and meat soup, please," he said.

Lady Matilda's shriek was even shriller this time. "Edward! I hope you're joking! After a trip like that Alvin will be tired out and his tummy will be upset. Isn't it true, my dear delicate little bundle of..."

"Matilda, please, I'm hungry," interrupted her husband.

"Excuse me Edward," she said. Then she addressed the waiter. "Bring me a half fillet of boiled sole with a little sauce Rémoulade."

A muffled groan came from under the table.

"Did you hear that?" asked Gea. "Alvin said «Uuumph»"

"He always says that," explained Lady Matilda, "when he's tired and his appetite's not very good."

"I think that «Uuumph»," Edward corrected her, "means simply: «For Heaven's sake, I'm starving, and just hear what they're going to feed me with!»"

The first course arrived, and Alvin had the microscopic meal his mistress had ordered put under his nose. With one accurate flick of his tongue, he took the little fish off the plate. He swallowed it, and with a second flick of his tongue he licked the plate clean. Once finished, there was nothing left for him to do but to sit and brood on life's sadness.

A little later he was just having a sniff at a corner of the table-cloth, to see whether it was in fact inedible, when he suddenly caught sight of a pack of dogs brawling over a bone on the far side of the little square.

At first Alvin looked at them with a rather patronizing good-humour, arching his eyebrows a little: they hadn't any manners, you could see that straight away, and there was no doubt about their origins, they'd obviously been born and bred in the gutter.

But little by little, as he watched them pushing and shoving and rolling on the pavement, he began to take a liking to them. They struck him as much more to his taste than the mincing, powdered dogs Lady Matilda kept introducing him to.

And when, with a masterly stroke, the smallest and skinniest dog in the pack managed to whip the bone away from the biggest of them, a huge tough who must have had a brown bear among his ancestors, Alvin felt his breast swell with enthusiasm.

He took a careful look at the bone they were fighting over: it looked dirty and repulsive and had hardly any meat left on it. Any well-brought-up dog that came across it would have made a detour round it with his nose in the air.

"I reckon I can't be so well-brought-up," Alvin said to himself, his mouth watering.

Keeping four rivals at bay with one paw, the brown bear had taken the bone away from the skinny dog again. Alvin quivered as he felt his ancestors' fighting and hunting instinct rising within him out of the dark mist of time.

In a flash he forgot his pedigree, hygiene, lady's perfume and good manners. Like a streak of lightning, he shot out from under the table, zoomed across the square and dived at full speed into the packs of dogs. With a growl worthy of a Bengal tiger his jaws snapped on the bone and tore it away from the brown bear.

The dogs were left open-mouthed. The raid had been so swift and unexpected that the poor things hadn't even caught a glimpse of the attacker's face.

They were still trying to fathom it out when one of their number who boasted of having a bloodhound as his great-grandfather began to waggle his nose. "Can't you smell it?" he asked the others, who had immediately started sniffing the air.

"I might be wrong, but it smells like lady's perfume to me," put in another dog who, since he belonged to a hotel doorkeeper, knew the smells and the perfumes of half the world.

A perfumed dog, and therefore a dog with deluxe breeding, well-cared-for and well-fed, who steals a large dirty

25

bone with the ability of a professional… Here was a case that just had to be investigated.

The brown bear didn't waste any time: he gave a howl and disappeared down the lane, followed by the whole gang.

A moment later three acquaintances of ours arrived at the gallop on the spot where the dogs had been: Lady Matilda, still clutching a napkin in her hand, Lord Edward, who had spilled a glass of wine down his shirt in the upheaval, and Gea.

"Alvin, Aaalvin!" Lady Matilda called, waving the napkin in the air as if it was a flag.

The three of them disappeared down the lane at full speed.

Chapter four

Having reached this point in our story, we must now go back a little and look closely at Edward, Matilda and Gea's long journey to Venice.

None of the three was aware of it, but from the moment they had driven into Switzerland right up to their arrival in Venice, a mysterious car had been following them, close enough not to lose sight of them but far enough behind not to cause suspicion.

Riding in that mysterious car there were three famous international crooks: Rubino, Volauvent and Muscleton.

As we said, it had all begun in Switzerland.

In peace and quiet the three crooks were enjoying a paltry week's holiday - this was as long as they could allow themselves - when, driving along a mountain road, they suddenly passed our friends' Rolls Royce going in the other direction.

"Good grief! It's Lord Peacock!" exclaimed Volauvent. "Stop, Rubino, turn the car round!"

"Nonsense," said Rubino calmly. "We're on holiday, work can wait."

"But Lord Peacock's rolling in money, I know he is!" Volauvent insisted. "His wife's got jewels that..."

"Jewels can wait, our holiday can't."

"I was just saying his wife's got jewels worth a million dollars!" Volauvent finished.

Rubino's right foot pounced on the brake: the tyres squealed on the asphalt and the car, heeling over like a ship in the storm, changed direction and began the pursuit.

Rubino, Volauvent and Muscleton were three strange-looking characters.

Nobody would have taken them for expert crooks: Rubino and Muscleton might have attracted suspicion - but as chicken thieves, petty criminals in a village, nothing more. As for Volauvent, he looked more like a country gentleman than a professional thief.

Rubino was small, thin as a rake, touchy and very fly. He had long black sideburns and under the shiny black lock of hair that came down from over his forehead, there glittered a pair of small foxy eyes: five minutes after shaving, his cheeks were already blue with fresh stubble.

He thought he was very elegant, and just to prove this he had fitted himself out, especially for this trip, with a white-striped blue suit, a yellow shirt, a large flower-pattern tie and a pair of very shiny pointed shoes.

It was hard to imagine that with his tiny babylike hands he could steal a watch by unfastening it from your wrist in a fraction of a second, or slip the notes out of your wallet while it was still in your pocket.

On long winter evenings, old crooks who have retired are fond of telling their grandchildren about Rubino's most famous exploits.

For example, they tell them about the time when Rubino, having cast greedy eyes on the Nabob of Ahmedabad's fingers, which were loaded with rings, introduced himself and shook hands: these few seconds were enough for Rubino to slip four diamonds rings off the Nabob's fingers.

They also tell of the time when, during a great ball in the Count of Wunsterberg's palace, Volauvent put out the lights for three seconds - time enough for Rubino to deprive the unsuspecting ladies of fourteen earrings, eight necklaces and twenty-four bracelets, not to speak of the gold watch that, soon after, he slipped off the police inspector who'd come to investigate.

As we said before, Volauvent was a real gentleman. Few men could rival his elegance when he wore spats and monocle, crocodile-leather shoes and damask-skill waistcoat, and carried his cane with his ivory top. Few were as refined as he was in their choices of wines, in kissing ladies' hands, or using a jade cigarette-holder. Light as a feather, he could dance a flawless tango.

It was thanks to his polished manners, to his acquaintances, and to his lightning imagination, that Rubino and Muscleton, almost always on the sly and at the last minute, managed to get into places frequented by society's élite - where they confidently brought off their amazing coups.

If Volauvent was the "mind", and Rubino the "hand" of the trio, Muscleton was without any doubt the "arm".

He was about as tall and wide as a middling-size wardrobe, yet genial and very gentle. In fact he wouldn't have hurt a fly.

He had a crew-cut hair which was carroty-red, and hands as large as tennis-rackets. His face was creased in an ingenuous smile. His right arm was embellished by a proud tattoo showing a galleon in full sail.

Even though his clothes were amusing and comfortable, they were far from elegant and often brought indignant protests from his two colleagues. He used to wear jeans and a red-and-white striped t-shirt, a sailor hat and a pair of tennis shoes.

While he might sometimes wear a t-shirt with different coloured stripes or a different-shaped hat, the ingredients of his clothing were always substantially the same.

You can easily imagine Muscleton's job. When the trio were faced with problems of transport, his contribution was decisive. Rubino and Volauvent were very grateful to him: they were always ready to admit that without him they would never have managed to carry four large suitcases full of silverware away from a Grand Hotel on the Côte d'Azur. And, thanks to Muscleton, raids on safes no longer offered special problems: they would get into the rooms where the safe was kept and, instead of fiddling about with the lock for hours, Muscleton would just put the safe under his arm and carry it away. They could take their time over opening it in their workshop.

However, just like everybody else, Muscleton had his faults, and the most dangerous of these was undoubtedly his excessive enthusiasm.

For example, during one of their nocturnal excursions, this time to the villa of a famous singer, he saw an ivory-white grand piano. He fell in love with it at first sight, and his companion pleaded with him in vain telling him that he was too old to learn to play such a difficult instrument and that with such thick fingers he would never be able to play one note at a time.

Luckily, the piano was too big to go through the door and it was only then that Muscleton gave up, his eyes glistening with disappointment.

As we said then, after seeing Lord Peacock's Rolls Royce, the three began to follow it, waiting for the moment when they could relieve Lady Matilda of her famous jewels.

The first stop the Peacoks made was on the shore of an Italian lake. They took rooms in a nice little Nineteenth-century hotel that was surrounded by willow trees. Rubino was dispatched to have a discreet look inside, but he came back unsatisfied.

"Too many staircases and wooden floors," he told his friends, shaking his head. "I don't like working with creaky floors all round me."

It was thus that the trio settled down not far from the hotel to wait for a more promising occasion. Rubino and Volauvent took advantage of the delay to bring up the usual old subject.

"Muscleton, your clothes are wrong," began Rubino.

"What do you mean *wrong*?" the giant asked. "First time on this trip you've had anything to say about 'em."

"Well, we were on holiday before," Volauvent explained, "and of course on holiday you can take certain liberties. But now we're working, and at work we must look serious and respectable."

"No doubt Lord Peacock will go to some high-class places," went on Rubino. "You can't go around dressed like that."

"You look like a cross between an escaped convict and a clown from a circus," Volauvent finished up.

Muscleton lowered his head. His bottom lip was sticking out and his chin quivering.

"Oh come on Muscleton, don't get upset," Volauvent tried to console him. "I didn't mean to hurt you."

"Of course," Rubino said to encourage him, and patted him on the shoulder. "Volauvent only wanted to tell you that if you turn up in the middle of respectable company dressed like that, they'll all slip away to check the police telephone number."

"You remember what happened last New Year's night?" sobbed Muscleton.

They both remembered only too well. The trio was in Paris. They'd gone to an important reception in the Argentine ambassador's residence and were counting on coming away with his valuable stamp collection. For this occasion, Rubino and Volauvent had spent half of a day persuading Muscleton to wear evening dress with tails

On arriving at the reception, the poor chap had held out by not breathing too deeply for almost an hour, but then, while he was dancing a waltz with Baroness Landowska, he got carried away: he made a couple of turns with her and then took a deep breath. His cloth burst like an overfull balloon, leaving him standing in striped vest and flower-pattern pants.

It caused such a scandal that the Paris newspapers talked about it for a week. And of course the stamp collection coup was out of the question.

"After all," Rubino reassured him, "this time you've no need to wear evening dress. You just need a normal suit."

"I can't find a suit to fit me," Muscleton mumbled.

"Just for once," Rubino said, "you ought to go and get yourself a suit made by a good upholsterer."

Volauvent pointed out that there was no time to lose and they should find a suit before evening because the following day might give them the chance to get their hands on the jewels.

The three of them ransacked all the shops in area and in the end, with a lot of patience and luck, they managed to find more or less what they were looking for.

The morning after, before they set out to follow the Peacocks' car, poor Muscleton had to imprison himself in a white shirt and tie, a chequered jacket and a pair of trousers that left six inches of bare leg visible above his shoes. He looked like a large pillow crammed into a tiny pillow-slip.

After a long drive in the wake of the Rolls Royce, the three reached Venice. At a distance they followed the Peacocks out of the garage, but when the little family handed their luggage over to the motorboat driver, they were too far away to read the hotel name on the boat's bow.

"Damn it," muttered Rubino. "I bet the jewels are in those suitcases!"

"I wonder what hotel they're going to…" Muscleton said to himself, straightening his shirt-collar which kept on curling up.

"We've got to choose," said Rubino. "Either we follow them or their suitcases."

"There is no hurry," Volauvent said decisively. "We'll follow the family."

Strolling through the city behind their quarry, they eventually reached the little square with the restaurant and hid in the shadow of a small lane, waiting for the Peacocks to finish their meal.

Muscleton was telling his companions how his eyes were growing dim with hunger, when suddenly the tourists' white and black dog flashed across the square, snatched the bone from the pack of dogs and scampered headlong down the very lane the trio were hiding in. A moment later an avalanche of dogs sped past them in pursuit of the bone. And the dogs were quickly followed by the Peacocks themselves.

"Full speed ahead, boys," hissed Volauvent, "or else we'll lose 'em!"

The three of them sprinted after the others.

The barking of the dogs, Lady Peacock's cries and Muscletone's lumbering footsteps gradually died away in the shadows of the little lanes, and silence reigned once again in the square.

Chapter five

High and imposing like a moving mountain, the ship plowed its way through the calm of the Adriatic Sea.

Its decks were packed with a carefree crowd. One group of passengers were enjoying the sunshine by the side of the swimming pool, while others were swimming. The laziest ones were gazing at the sea from their deckchairs, many were strolling about the decks or taking photos.

Leaning over the rail at the stern, one young boy had been long watching a group of dolphins who were swimming and jumping by the ship's side.

The boy's name was Gianni, and he was the son of the famous film director Antonio Ferreri.

Among all the dolphins, who now and then leapt out of the water, Gianni had finally managed to single out who was larger and seemed lighter than the others: he rode the waves with the grace of a ballerina, leapt in a perfect half-moon arc out of the water and plunged back below the waves without raising the slightest splash.

The boy heard his own name called and looked round: it was his father.

"Dad, come and have a look," he said. When the man was beside him, he pointed out the dolphins. "Look, look at him!" he shouted. "He is the cleverest of them all! Oh... isn't he beautiful?"

His father leaned over the rail beside him and watched the dolphin flickering in the water. "He's really wonderful..." he said. "They're following the ship for the fun of it, just to make a show."

"Look, look again!" the boy exclaimed. "Did you see him?"

"Yes, you're right, he's a fantastic jumper."

"I'll call him Silverskin!" said Gianni. "Dad, would you like to be a dolphin?"

The man smiled. "I think I would," he replied.

They stood there in silence for a minute, looking at the dolphins' wonderful show.

Then Gianni asked: "Why did you call me just now?"

"Oh yes, I'd forgotten. I wanted to tell you that we're getting near Venice."

"Are we really? Can you see it yet?"

"With a pair of binoculars you can see the highest roofs, church domes and bell towers."

Gianni and his father left the rail and went up to the next deck, the one below the funnels.

Venice gradually came into view. Its buildings covered a large stretch of the horizon and looked like a gigantic fleet of galleons.

The first seagull appeared in the sky.

As the land came nearer, more and more passengers crowded onto the decks to gaze at the city they had come to visit.

"Look, there's the Lido," Gianni's father said to him, pointing to a vast expanse of sand with many-coloured cabins, trees and large hotels standing behind it. "It's the beach of Venice, and it's in one of those palaces that the Film Festival's going to be held."

"When are they going to show your film?" the boy asked.

"In three days' time."

"I bet you win the Golden Lion again."

"And I bet you'll get bored to death!" said the man, smiling. "Anyhow I promise that as soon as the Festival's over we'll have a week to ourselves. We'll take a motorboat and visit all the islands in the lagoon, and have a good tour round Venice. All right?"

"That's wonderful, dad," Gianni said, pretending to believe what his father had said.

Of course he knew his father wouldn't want to tell him lies, he really wanted to do all those things with him as soon as the Festival's was over. But then, Gianni knew from experience, what really happened would be quite different. Dad was too important and until the very moment they left Venice he would be surrounded from morning to night by an invincible army of journalists, producers, photographers, autograph-hunters, actors and actresses.

Gianni himself would have to stay out of the way waiting for the storm to calm down. But it was his father's job, with its good and its bad points like any other job, so Gianni didn't let himself get down in the mouth even if he was often left alone.

The ship's siren boomed out loudly. The noise broke his train of thoughts and made him turn back to reality around him.

The ship was now passing between two lighthouses, each of which stood at the end of a very long quay stretching out into the sea. It was skirting low-lying strips of land and islands covered with trees.

Finally it entered the lagoon in the middle of which rose the city of Venice. The vast landscape was solemn, but at the same time gentle.

The fishing-ship's red and yellow sail seemed to be sleeping above the still waters. Scattered all over the immense lagoon around these ships, there were countless piles jutting out of the water to mark off the labyrinth of channels.

Here and there the low tide had uncovered thin strips of land and with hoarse cries the seagulls were diving down on these, stretching out their beaks in search of food.

Little by little Gianni saw the city spread out before him. The houses and the gardens ran down to an extremely long quay which was interrupted occasionally by bridges. Crowds of people could be seen moving up and down the quay. In the distance towards the centre of the city one could see the dome of churches, the Ducal Palace, the St Mark's Basilica, one of the most beautiful Italian cathedrals, and its huge campanile, the highest bell-tower in Venice.

Attracted by the view of the Lido, the appearance of the lagoon, and the city itself, Gianni had not glanced at the sea to the ship's stern, and like him, all the other passengers had turned their gaze towards the land.

The dolphins, realizing that no one was watching their acrobatics any more, had got offended. Disappointed, they made their way towards the open sea again.

Instead, the smartest of them all, Silverskin, had not given up. Piqued by his jealousy of what the passengers were looking at, he had tried to regain their admiration by increasing the number and the length of his leaps and pirouetting two or three times before diving back.

He had got so absorbed in these acrobatics that he had not even realized where the ship was leading him.

When he suddenly caught sight of the coloured sails, the launches and the houses not far away, he gave a last frightened twist in the air and disappeared under the water.

He came up again soon after but only pocked his head out of the water. Just enough, in fact, to have a look round.

He glimpsed the city and at once understood why there had been no admirers for his marvellous leaps.

With a flick of annoyance, he made as if to turn back towards the open sea. But then his curiosity got the better of him and he felt irresistibly drawn towards the luminous buildings that were reflected in the water.

And while the ship turned its stern towards the harbour, the dolphin dived under the surface, and swimming fast, disappeared in the direction of the city.

Chapter six

Phoebus, the carrier-pigeon who had come to Venice shortly before, and his now inseparable friend, were perching on a branch of an ancient and majestic plane-tree which stood at the foot of a bell-tower

There, in the cool green shade, Phoebus had been resting after his long flight, lulled by the cheerful voices of the boys in the square below, the humming of the wind through the branches and the twittering of the sparrows.

Then, from the campanile, a heavy bell had started booming out and his friend had called to him.

"Phoebus, if you want to get there in time, we'd better go," he said him.

"In time for what?" the carrier-pigeon asked, with a slight start.

"In time to listen the Lion's stories. If you still want to that is."

"Why, of course," Phoebus had replied with a smile.

For a moment he'd forgotten he was in Venice. Waking up suddenly like that had made him think he was still on a mission.

With a swoop they had left the branches and flown out into the sunshine. And now they were winging over the city.

Below them, in all directions, there lay a sea of roofs, many of which were adorned by small terraces shaped like arbours. All these terraces where brightened by the colours of flowers

The wind was fluttering the washing on the terrace clothes-lines.

"You see, space is precious in Venice," his friend explained. "With those roof-terraces the Venetians can enjoy all the space of the sky. Centuries ago, the ladies used to go up to those terraces to undo their hair, so that it would take on the red and gold tints of the sunset. And in the evening the terraces were lit with small coloured lanterns, and the people would talk and sing to the accompaniment of lutes…"

Suddenly t near to the sea?" hey saw St Mark's Square gleaming below them.

Phoebus looked at the two great marble palaces and to the high bell tower.

"The palace at the right is the Doge's Palace, the residence of the Duke of Venice," his friend said. "Do you see those two columns near to the sea?"

Phoebus nodded.

"Well, our friend the Lion stands just on top of the right column!

They came down swiftly and perched on top of the winged Lion's column. Many birds had already gathered on the pedestal.

After staring at Phoebus for a moment, the Lion asked him: "But weren't you supposed to leave at once?"

"I should have, but…" Phoebus replied with a sigh.

One of the pigeons finished the sentence for him: "… but Venice had conquered him. An so have your stories, Mr Lion."

"I understand, I'd better start then," the statue said, while the birds arranged themselves in order in front of him. "What would you like me to talk about?"

"My friends had told me a few things that have made me curious," Phoebus said. "What was Venice like long ago?"

"Not very different from the way it is now," began the Lion. "All the things that had changed the appearance of other ancient cities, such as cars, neon signs, traffic lights. traffic noises, skyscrapers, have never come to Venice. Only the people have changed, at least their clothes and their habits have. Nowadays the Venetians live much more simply and modestly than they used to. But once…"

The Lion stopped for a while, as if trying to recall everything he had seen over the centuries.

"Four hundred years ago, for example," he went on, "Venice was the richest, the most splendid city in the world. The nobles' palaces contained rich cloths, valuable inlaid furniture, and many things in gold and silver. Till late into the night, behind the palace windows with their many-coloured panes, you could see the glow of the lights for banquets and receptions. In the city streets there was a continual to and fro of people of all races an nations - merchants from the East, sailors, travellers, soldiers, clergymen, hawkers and peasants. Yet none of them attracted as much attention as the noble ladies and the gentlemen of Venice. They would walk slowly, as proud and magnificent as queens and kings, showing off the luxury of their clothes in brocade, silk, damask and velvet, and displaying the splendour of the ornaments they wore: precious stones, pearls, exotic plumes, lace, pendants furs, swords and daggers.

But to get a real idea of the riches and wonders of Venice, you should have seen one of the public celebrations that the city enjoyed during the course of a year. Only the palette of the great painters has been able to portrait effectively the solemn religious processions, the Carnival celebrations, the ceremonies for the crowning of the Doge, the triumphal welcome given to the famous men, the tournaments and the joustings on horseback, the celebrations of military victories, the regattas, the fireworks, the serenades on the water by the light of thousands of Chinese lanterns…"

"It must have been wonderful to see sights like that!" exclaimed one of the birds. "You were very lucky, Mr Lion."

"Ah yes, of course I was," the statue admitted, "even if, on many nights of the year, I couldn't get a wink of sleep..."

"Mr Lion, you said they used to have tournaments and joustings on horseback in Venice," Phoebus remarked. "But did they have horses in Venice? How could the horses go up and down the steps on the bridges?"

"Up until the Sixteenth century there used to be lots and lots of horses in Venice," the Lion answered. "The bridges were not humpbacked as they are now, but flat and without steps. The only precaution that the Venetian riders had to take was to put bells on their horses so that the people swarming in the lanes could hear them coming and stand aside in time. The Venetian nobles were so fond of riding that they didn't even dismount when they had to enter their places: the flight of steps were built so that the horses could mount them.

You could even ride up to the top of the campanile, i.e. the bell-tower of St Mark's on horseback by means of a spiral ramp. The Venetians were so proud of this that in 1452 they got the German emperor Fredrick III to ride up to the top. And what an odd business that was: a German emperor on the back of his charger standing, so to speak, in the sky over Venice...

Ah yes, perhaps it's because they live in such a strange city, but the Venetian have always had a liking for the odd and the eccentric. The most elegant of the nobles, for example, would use a colour they obtained from a plant - brought from the distant island of Cyprus - to dye their horses bright orange. No wonder the girls would rush to the windows to gaze at them as soon as they heard the horse-bells approaching..."

"I'd say there's no animal in the world vainer than man," remarked a pigeon. "What do you think, Mr Lion?"

The Lion's great mouth twisted in an ironic smile. "As far as I've seen, I'd say there's one animal vainer than man: and that's woman."

The birds twittered with amusement.

Then Phoebus put another question to the Lion. "Were the Venetians happier then or now?"

"It's hard to say," the statue answered. "Today they don't have, in their way of life, any of their past glory or splendour, but on the other hand they don't have to face the mystery, the fears and the dangers that once surrounded them. Venice at night was completely dark. Only here and there you could see the dim flickering little lights placed at the foot of holy statues. The darkness was ideal cover for plots, attacks, conspiracies and duels.

Such things were so frequent that in 1450 a law was passed which said that whoever went out at night had to carry a candle or a torch to light the way. In those times the nobles used to have a servant with a light in his hand walking in front of them whenever they went out in the dark. But as you might imagine the new law didn't make the darkness any safer for the Venetians."

"At times like that," a pigeon said with a shudder, "it's better to stay perched high up in a tree or on a statue!"

"True enough," said the Lion, "but you mustn't think all Venetians were afraid of a moonless night! Many of them were born with a natural love of adventures and risk-taking. What a lot of travellers, warriors and discoverers I've seen sail from that quay down there!

Eight hundred years ago Marco Polo embarked there. He was the great traveller who went to explore lands known until then only to Arabian and Asiatic caravan-leaders. He crossed fascinating and awe-inspiring countries like Persia, Turkestan and Mongolia, and after three year's travelling, thousands of miles from home, he finally reached the Land of Mystery: China.

And it was from this quay that the Venetian Giovanni Caboto, whose name was translated in England John Cabot, set sail. At first he went to England, then, in 1497, he left Bristol on a small ship, similar to the caravel of Columbus, with a crew of eighteen men, and took the flag of St Mark's to Newfoundland, Labrador and Canada.

And a few years later his son Sebastian sailed from Venice and discovered Florida, explored Hudson Bay and went up to the great South American river, the Paraguay. As a reward for his courage, the English king Edward VI appointed him "Governor for life of the Merchant Adventurers".

Many other daring Venetian seamen set out from here to seek unknown lands, and among them there was Alvise Cadamosto, who explored the Atlantic coast of Africa and discovered the Island of Cape Verde. Many of these explorers never returned, but some came back with fantastic treasures…"

The Lion paused and watched the tourists coming and going in the square. How the people of Venice had changed…

"My friends, I think it's enough for today," he said after a thinking for a few moment. "Next time I'll tell you… well, I'll tell you something about the public celebrations in Venice. What about that?"

A cooing of approval went up from the group of birds.

"In the meantime," the Lion suggested to the pigeons, "you could take our new friend Phoebus to meet the other statues. If I'm not mistaken, the Archangel Gabriel there on the top of St Mark's campanile knows some very nice stories…"

In the meantime, at the foot of the Lion's column, a group of tourist pointed the gleaming eyes of their cameras up in the air.

The Lion saw them, and lifted his nose up in the air, raising high his wings and tails.

Soon his photos would be stuck proudly in many family albums.

Chapter seven

Alvin, clenching the bone he'd stolen from the gang of dogs between his jaws, was running headlong through the shaded lanes, skilfully avoiding the groups of boys who tried to stop him when they saw him coming.

It was a long time since he'd done anything as enjoyable and exhilarating as this. To be precise, not since two years before, when he was still a puppy and had made the stately ambassador of the Principality of Walchenstein trip up in a tearoom in Baden-Baden, sending him sprawling, medals and all, onto a trolley loaded with custard-pies.

It was a joy for him to let his legs carry him where they liked, diving down lanes so narrow that two people couldn't have walked abreast in them, scampering through the darkness of secret passages, dangerously skirting the edges of canals, and bounding up and down the steps on the bridges.

When he thought he'd left his pursuers far enough behind, he slowed down and finally found a quiet little spot at the bottom of a lane, where he laid the bone on the ground.

After having a good look at it, he had to admit that it really wasn't worth very much. Without conviction he started to gnaw it, just so that nobody could say he'd stolen it for nothing. Then, when there wasn't a trace of meat left on it, he sat down.

He was just considering how to make the best use of his freedom, when, from the lane on the right, he heard a confused scampering noise together with frantic panting. A second later, the gang of dogs rushed into sight.

When the dog who was in the lead saw Alvin, he immediately splayed out his legs to speed and came to a halt. His companions piled behind him, losing their balance and tumbling over one another.

When they recovered, they saw that Alvin was still there, sitting motionless and looking at them with an amused smile.

They took a few steps toward him, sniffing, and then stopped at a respectable distance. They obviously found this strange fellow in front of them rather curious, and a bit worrying.

"How did you manage to find me?" Alvin asked cheerfully.

One of his pursuers, in fact the one who boasted a bloodhound great-grandfather, approached him sniffing noisily. "The perfume," he said.

"Lady's perfume," added the hotel dog. "*Séduction*, or *Mon désir*, I should think."

"*Mon désir*, damn it!" muttered Alvin. "Is it very strong?"

"As you can see, we've traced you," pointed out the bloodhound mongrel.

"What a disgrace…" sighed Alvin, lowering his gaze. "You must think I'm one of those nagging little brutes that spend the day curled up on old ladies' sofas…"

"Judging from the business with the bone, I wouldn't say so," remarked one of the gang. "Perfumed dogs usually look down their noses at bones."

"I was hungry," Alvin explained. "My mistress puts me on a diet every so often. Any normal dog couldn't feel satisfied after eating just a slice of sole with *sauce Rémoulade*."

"Yes, but you shouldn't grumble," put in one of the gang, a kind of dachshund with yellowish fur. "Just think that what you eat on the other days, a luxury dog like you…"

"Always the same stuff, don't think it's anything special," replied Alvin. "Partridge *à la normande*, fillet of veal with truffles, chicken breast *à la viennoise*, ham with melon, *purée* of asparagus, peaches and cream… They even give me pineapple ice-cream! I ask you: can a dog go eating food like that all the time?"

The dogs were simply standing there with gaping mouths, their gaze lost in a distant, impossible dream.

"Could you eat stuff like that every day?" insisted Alvin, quivering with indignation.

"Yes, I could," gurgled the thinnest of the pack, his mouth watering.

"You ought to try, you'd soon change your mind!" Alvin exclaimed, pointing a paw at him. "I've spent many a night dreaming of simple food like bread and milk, potato soup, and a bone to gnaw. Then in the morning, I'd wake up and there would be the butler standing in front of me with tea and a tray of little cakes. But you understand my problem now, don't you?"

"No…" groaned the bloodhound mongrel, licking his whiskers.

"Nobody understands me," Alvin said sadly, and getting up, began to walk away.

At once, the dogs crowded round him.

"We didn't want to offend you," one of them said. "Really, we didn't…"

"If you stay with us," another tempted him, "you can count on getting a few bones or a plate of rice and beans. And we'll show you round Venice too…"

Alvin stopped in his tracks, struck by a sudden inspiration. "Another thing I've always dreamed of," he said, "is stealing a great long sausage. Do you think I could do it?"

The dogs put their heads together for a few moments, then one of them explained to him: "It's not easy, each of us has tried at least once, and the shopkeepers keep their eyes skinned. But with a bit of luck…"

"I've got you," said Alvin. "Let's go."

The gang moved off.

As they trotted down the lanes, each of the dogs in turn introduced himself. The small group consisted of Cicero, a dog who knew a lot about Venice - he had learned most of it by poking round his master's bookshop; Sniffy the bloodhound mongrel; Beppo, the biggest of them all; Casanova, the hotel dog; Lindoro, Lemon, Ali Baba, and Crumb, who was the smallest.

"Shall I tell you something about Venice?" Cicero asked his new friend at once. "I could explain the Duke's policy in Fourteenth-century Venice, for example, if you liked."

"Hmmm..." answered Alvin.

"Well then," Cicero insisted, "what about artistic trends in Venetian sculpture of the Eighteenth century?"

"Brrr..." said Alvin.

"But is there anything in Venice that interests you?" implored Cicero,

"Sausages," the fox-terrier replied implacably.

"Come on Alvin, don't be nasty," put in Beppo. "Let him talk a bit..."

"Some little historical titbit, eh?" Cicero said tentatively.

Resigned, Alvin gave him a nod. As they were walking along the side of a canal that was crowded with boats, Cicero, happy at last, began to talk.

"As you've noticed," he said, looking at Alvin, "the streets in Venice aren't real streets like those in other cities. That's why Venetians don't call them streets or roads, but *calli*, which comes from the Latin *callis*. Do you know what *callis* means in Latin?"

"No," muttered Alvin.

"It means lane, or path," Cicero explained beaming with happiness. "In fact the streets of Venice are narrow and winding just like country lanes.

There are lots and lots of these lanes in Venice, about 3000 of them, and they make a real maze where you can easily get lost if you don't know the town. Besides these lanes, Venice is criss-crossed by canals, a hundred and seventy-seven of them, and there are four hundred bridges over them.

The bridges used to be made of wood without steps and without parapets, but nowadays, as you've seen, they're nearly all of stone. Another important thing in Venice is…"

Cicero never finished the sentence. All of a sudden, Sniffy, the bloodhound mongrel, had stopped with his nose pointing in the air and had whispered: "Halt… quiet! There's an unmistakable smell… sausages!"

Eighteen ravenous eyes swept the horizon. In the distance, at the bottom of the lane, hanging on a shop-door, there was a superb sausage swinging gently in the breeze.

A long whine of pleasure rose from the gang, and several tails started wagging.

"No, wait a minute boys," said Cicero. "You'd better forget about that shop. I know the shopkeeper: he's so big that he has to walk sideways when he's going down some of the city lanes. And just look how high that sausage is!"

"I'm on holiday," Alvin asserted, "I want to live dangerously."

"A Pomeranian I know has already tried to steal a sausage from that shop," said Cicero. "Well, he fell into the shopkeeper's clutches and came back home with a muzzle that looked like a bulldog's."

"Follow me," ordered Alvin, now deaf to all advice.

Creeping along, the gang came up to within a few doors of the shop.

There was the sausage, rich brown, smelling delicious, and dangling invitingly. It seemed like a sphinx that said to passing dogs: "Come on, you nice little fellows, jump up and take me. But watch out: if you don't get me, you'll be in trouble…"

"Now listen carefully to what I say," Alvin whispered to the gang. "Go as near as you can to the shop, without being seen of course, and line up one behind the other."

Cicero let out a groan. "Now I know what you are," he said. "You're nuts!"

"Let him finish," grumbled Lemon.

"You must line up tallest first shortest last," went on Alvin. "Crumb, you're the smallest, you go at the back of the line. Lindoro, you come after Crumb, and then the others, finishing with Beppo, who's the biggest. He'll be nearest the shop."

"That's great, if the man comes out I'll get the first swipe from him!" Beppo protested.

"There won't be any hitches, you'll see," Alvin reassured him. "And remember all of you: as soon as you see me with the sausage in my mouth, take off!"

At a sign from Alvin, who now seemed to have become their leader, the dogs began to creep cautiously towards the enemy's line. You could see that Cicero and a couple of others had got a fit of the shakes.

At the moment the lane was deserted. There was absolute silence.

The dogs lined up as they had been told and stood waiting.

Alvin walked back a few paces, took a lightning run-up and sprang lightly and nimbly onto Crumb's back, then Lindoro's, Cicero's, Lemon's and the others, higher and higher until he reached Beppo's mighty shoulders, from which, leaping like a gazelle, he flew, literally flew, at the sausage.

The huge man in the shop, who had nothing to do at that moment, was sitting behind the counter looking towards the window.

Suddenly he saw a streak of lightning shaped like a dog fly past the window at an impossible height, and a second later the sausage had disappeared. For a moment he thought it was a dream and stayed stock-still, looking upwards with his mouth wide open. He only came to when he saw a small gang of dogs rushing past, this time at ground level and one behind the other in order of height.

For the moment he didn't try to understand. He just grabbed the first weapon that came to hand - in his haste he picked up the little brush used for dusting the counter - and charged out of the shop.

The dogs were a long way from the shop by now. His sausage was bobbing along at the head of the group like a victory flag waving in the wind.

The shopkeeper could do nothing but stamp his feet and launch terrible threats at the retreating thieves, threats that would have seemed even more frightening if he had been brandishing something more warlike than a little brush.

Gradually the lane filled with women who had heard the shouting and wanted to know what it was all about. They gathered around the furious shopkeeper and began arguing about what had happened. The Stolen Sausage would certainly be the topic of the day for them.

But let's go back to Alvin and his companions.

After a couple of minutes' frantic flight, the gang with Cicero in the lead turned down a quiet lane. At the end of this they came out on the banks of a canal which they followed for a few yards, and then all took shelter in a solitary fishing boat moored on the canal.

The boat's hold, which was in half-darkness, was cosy and safe. The dogs crouched down on the nets and put the sausage in the middle of the circle they had formed. Then they shared out the sausage.

Alvin noticed with astonishment that although there were now nine dogs in the gang including himself, Beppo had divided the sausage into ten parts. Naturally, he asked Beppo why.

"It's for the chief of the cats," Beppo explained.

Alvin stared at him with eyes as big as apricots.

"That's it, for the chief of the cats," Cicero repeated. "What's wrong with that?"

"Where I come from, us dogs don't treat cats so well," said Alvin, pointing his nose proudly in the air.

"You can afford not to," Cicero returned, "but we can't. The fact is that Venice would already have disappeared if it wasn't for the cats. It's a sad thing for a dog to admit, but that's the way it is. No… don't look at me like that, Alvin… I'm not mad. Listen a minute and you'll see I'm right.

Venice is built on millions of wooden piles driven into the bottom of the lagoon. So, if it there weren't any cats to patrol the city, the rats and mice would have multiplied time out of number and would have been able over so many centuries to gnaw through the wooden piles not once but an hundred times. If the cats hadn't been there to defend it, the city would be under water by now. You see what I mean?"

"I see alright!" Alvin exclaimed. "So you…"

"In fact," admitted Cicero, "we have to handle them with velvet gloves, give 'em presents, smile, always be kind and polite, never forget to call them «Sir» or «Madam»… To tell the truth, when it's a question of cats, there's no democracy for us anymore. Last Christmas, if you can believe it, we had to decorate a tree with hundreds of sardines for them. And a few months ago, when Cato's tenth birthday came around, we had to steal a cheesecake from a delicatessen and send it as a present with birthday candles on it."

"Who is this *Cato*?" asked Alvin.

"The Chief, the Boss, the Prince of the Venetian cats," went on Cicero. "He's so big and sleek that now he only haunts mice and rats as a sport, like millionaires hunting lions in Africa. Haven't you noticed what a lot of cats there are in Venice?"

"No, I haven't," replied Alvin. "Since I arrived I've done nothing but run."

"Well, if you look around you'll see there are at least three cats for every Venetian. People are so fond of cats that they wear cat's masques at carnival."

Crumb, who was licking his whiskers which still melt of sausage, intervened in the discussion: "There's another reason why dogs, specially little ones like me, ought to be careful about treating the cats in this town well," he said. "And it's a simple reason. Maybe it's because of the special treatment they had for centuries, but they're about twice as big as the other cats in other towns. Beppo, who weighs eighty pounds, could get away with being a bit rude to them. But I wouldn't try, I can tell you."

"I'd like to meet this Cato," said Alvin, a nasty smile lurking round the corner of his mouth.

Cicero looked at him in alarm and hurriedly asked: "Alvin, for heaven's sake, what do you want to do?"

"Nothing in particular," answered Alvin. "I'd just like to meet him, that's all."

"The cats of Venice are sacred like those in Ancient Egypt, remember?" Cicero warned him. Then, after a pause, he added: "I'll introduce you only on condition that you promise to call him «Sir» and behave politely."

"Agreed," murmured Alvin, rather reluctantly.

They all left the hold of the boat and set off to visit Cato. Crumb took the lead with Cato's piece of sausage held gingerly between his teeth.

As they plodded on, Alvin noticed that the lanes they went through were getting more and more crowded and noisy. He could hear a far-off buzzing and bustling like the sound of bees seething round a hive. His curiosity aroused, Alvin quickened his pace and trotted to the front of the group.

"Keep close to us or you'll get lost," Cicero warned him.

"Where are we going then?" Alvin asked.

"To the Rialto market. We'll find Cato and his subjects there."

They turned into a lane at the bottom of which they could see a lot of people bustling to and fro. As they came up with this crowd, they were plunged into a small picturesque world full of colours, noises, lights and busy movement.

On the market stalls, in harmonious disorder, they saw gorgeous cascades of peaches, tomatoes, green and purple figs, carrots, aubergines, melons, green, pink and black grapes, cauliflowers, beetroots and beans. Further on, chickens, sausages and various cheeses were on display. Other stalls presented flower seeds and poultry feed, wooden tools, bags, clothes and a thousand other articles. And round all these, stalls swirled a lively and inquisitive crowd.

"Maybe you'll find it's hard to believe," Cicero shouted in Alvin's ear, "but for some centuries the Rialto market was the centre of world trade. All the valuable goods from the East and the known lands of the time, like gold ware, silks, precious stones, and spices, came to the Rialto, and here merchants from all over Europe made their bids for them. Cicero stopped and looked round to make sure that none of the gang had got lost in the crowd, then he turned to Alvin again. "You really want to meet Cato and the other cats then?"

Alvin nodded.

Cicero warned him once again to be polite and respectful. Then all together they slipped under the fruit and vegetables stalls to reach the part of the market where fish was sold.

Here, in a quiet corner amidst soft cuttlefish, fleshy basses and bluish sardines, Cato the cat reigned supreme.

In spite of his promise to Cicero, Alvin in his heart of hearts had not completely given up the idea of making Cato's fur fly.

But when he saw him, he changed his mind.

Cato was sitting on a box, as solemn and stately as a king on his throne. His build was more or less that of a young puma, and he was covered with the typical gray and brown fur of tabby cats. He had long whiskers, which stuck out, and his ears were erect, sharp and sensitive. In the centre of his wide face, just above his pink nose, there gleamed two large topazes. At his feet there lay numerous fish scales. Next to these, sprawling lazily on some sacks, there were the cats of his retinue.

Cicero approached him and said: "Mr Cato, please accept our respectful greetings. We've brought you a small gift. If you can see your way to accepting this…"

Crumb came forward and laid the piece of sausage on the box in front of Cato. The latter looked at it, his nose twitched, and he gave a quick nod to a large black cat.

Immediately the black cat took the gift and put it one side, then he explained to Cicero: "His Excellency has just eaten. He will see later whether the sausage is to his liking."

"Mr Cato," said Cicero, gesturing to Alvin, "I would like to introduce a new friend of ours. He was the one that stole the sausage we brought you."

Alvin approached the box-throne. In tense ominous silence, the fox-terrier an the Prince of the Cats scrutinized each other.

Cato was strong, sly, and as impassive as an Egyptian mummy. After a few seconds' silence, he began twitching the tip of his tail.

Alvin felt a slight nudge in the ribs. It was Cicero, who whispered desperately in his ear: "Say «Hello»… say «Hello» for heaven's sake! Can't you see his tail is starting to wag?"

"Hi," Alvin said reluctantly out of the corner of his mouth.

Cato's tail began drumming on the box.

"No, no… not like that!" hissed Cicero, digging him sharply in the ribs. "Say «Good-day Sir» or we're in trouble!"

Alvin suddenly lost his temper.

Good God! He'd been able to take a bone away from an entire gang of dogs and steal a sausage from the most terrifying shopkeeper in Europe, and now he was supposed to bow and scrape to this ugly self-important cat!

He stuck his muzzle out towards Cato, wrinkled his nose and forehead and, before his guardian angel could stop him, pocked out his tongue as far as it would go.

What followed all took place in about twenty seconds.

Faced with such an unheard-of outrage, Cato leapt to his feet, drew his paws together, and arched his back, while the hairs on his back and his tail stood up stiff and straight. Then he started snarling and spitting with all the strength of his lungs.

"Good grief, run for it!" groaned poor Cicero breathlessly.

Alvin, feeling worried, put his tongue back in and turned just in time to see that his companions, instead of backing him up, were walking off as fast as they could.

And who could blame them? Alarmed by Cato's screeching, the fishmongers, the fruiterers and the cheese-sellers were rushing to his aid.

They would not have anyone ill-treating or even just annoying their precious cats, for heaven's sake!

With dismay, Alvin saw that he was about to be trampled down by something very like the Charge of the Light Brigade. He shot his tongue out once again at Cato, accompanying it with a resounding "Yah!", then darting among baskets, the fruit-boxes and the legs of the passers-by, he whipped off in pursuit of his companions.

His visit to Venice was definitely getting more and more like a sprint around a race-track.

As we saw, Lord Edward, Lady Matilda and Gea had to break off their meal and give chase to their restless runaway dog. Shadowed, as you know, by Rubino, Volauvent and Muscleton, the three unfortunate tourists ran on for quite a way looking in every nook and cranny for signs of their pet.

In the end, dead-tired and above all convinced that there was no trace of Alvin to be found, they slowed down and began to walk at a normal pace.

Gradually, almost without realizing it, they began to look at the things around them, stopping more and more often to gaze fascinated at all the marvellous sights the city was offering them.

They stared at the palaces full to overflowing with statues, the secret gardens hidden among the houses, the humble little churches and the decorated basilicas like huge climbing rose-plants. They watched the careful movements of the craftsmen in their shops, the boatmen rowing on the canals, the children playing in the sunshine in the squares, and the men playing cards at the tables of the bars.

By now they were fascinated by Venice. Its silence, its peaceful little squares, the simplicity of its people had made them forget the hard world of rush and worry in which they lived.

Lady Matilda, who had even forgotten her beloved Alvin, discovered that at the sides of the lanes there were enchanting shops full of sparkling glassware, antiques, silks and lace, jewels and decorated leathers. At every shop window she let out little shrieks of joy to call her husband's attention, but he was now busy with his camera and couldn't pay attention to her calls.

Gea began to take a serious interest in the windows of the ice-cream shops, and soon after brought her investigation to a successful conclusion by buying a big ice-cream cone.

Wandering along the lanes, they at last came out to a gleaming square.

Edward arranged his wife and daughter in suitable poses and began to get his camera ready.

The three thieves, who till then had never lost sight of the family, also turned up in the square. To keep up appearances, Rubino went up to a flower-seller's stall and began to smell the Canterbury bells, the dahlias and the gladioli, now and then stealing a glance at the Peacocks. The poor flower-seller was so taken aback at his behaviour that she did not even dare to ask him whether he wanted to buy anything.

For want of anything better to do, Muscleton tried to bend down and stroke a cat, but as the suit he was encased in started making sinister ripping noises, and in any case the cat withdrew in fright, he had to straighten up at once. So he went to a newspaper kiosk, bought a paper and, absentmindedly holding it upside down, pretended to read it.

As for Volauvent, he went into an antique shop and started pocking about among the candlesticks and statuettes, occasionally peering through his monocle to see what was going outside.

All of a sudden, just as Edward was on the point of taking the photo, a loud and powerful voice reached them from a nearby lane, soon followed by a subdued chattering from other people.

A terrible suspicion flashed through Edward's mind.

"Come with me," he stuttered, gesturing to Matilda and Gea, and striding towards the lane.

Rubino abandoned the flowers, Muscleton folded the paper up and put it in his pocket, and Volauvent rushed out of the antique shop, cursing the bad luck that had brought him away just when he was about to pocket up a Sixteenth-century medallion right under the unsuspecting antique-dealer's nose.

Lord Edward's suspicions were justified: that huge man shouting fit to bust and brandishing a ridiculous little brush, was going on about a black and white dog that had stolen a long sausage from him.

"Alvin," Edward whispered to his wife, and at once pushed his way through the crowd of chattering women and began to run in the direction that the huge man was pointing.

An instant later the three thieves followed on his trail. The terrifying shopkeeper, on seeing the three of them running up, became suspicious and thought they might be the owners of the dog that had robbed him.

"Hey, you there, stop a minute," he ordered Muscleton, shoving a fist as big as a football under his nose. "Have you got a small black and white dog by any chance, with a square muzzle and a tail sticking up in the hair?"

Muscleton, who, you remember, would not hurt a fly, took fright at being threatened by a man who was about as big as himself. What's more, he didn't want to lose track of the Peacocks.

He stammered something out and then, with a bound that jeopardized the life of his skin-tight trousers, he dashed off and caught up with his companions.

Of course, when he did this, all hell broke loose.

"It's him! It's him! The owner of the sausage-stealing dog!" yelled the shopkeeper, and quick as a flash the crowd of women parted to let him charge after his only chance of being paid for the stolen sausage.

There's no doubt the Peacocks had never spent such an eventful and animated holiday.

Chapter eight

Gianni, the boy we met on the ship coming into Venice, and his father, the famous film director, took their place on a motor launch soon after landing from the ship. Thus they crossed the lagoon and quickly reached the Lido.

Here, as happened every year, the International Film Festival was being held and Gianni's father, as you remember, was taking part in it.

The Lido welcomed them with its gleaming buildings, its wide avenues, its lively crowd and the noise of its traffic.

Gianni was surprised to see cars there. His father explained that they were carried there by car-ferries and that they could easily drive along the island with its wide asphalt roads.

After passing a line of taxis, they came to a horse-cab drowsing in the shade of a tree. The man looked enquiringly at the boy, who at once accepted the invitation very willingly. After putting their luggage next to the cab-driver, they climbed up and sat down on the comfortable seat.

"Let's go, Romeo!" shouted the driver, shaking gently the reins. The cab, rocking slightly, moved forward.

They turned into a long tree-lined avenue at the side of which stood souvenir shops, bars, new-stands, restaurants, gardens and villas. You could tell by the light, colourful clothes of the people, that the beach was nearby.

In fact they soon reached a large square beyond which stretched the sea. Then they turned right and presently arrived in front of a large hotel.

There were a lot of people in the entrance. Most of them were journalists, photographers, or actors. Many came forward to meet the new arrivals, bombarding the man with questions and taking innumerable photos. But both man and boy were tired and wanted to rest. So they escaped from the crowd and reached their room as fast as they could.

They woke up a couple of hours later. Someone was knocking on the door.

It was Robert Webster, the famous film producer. They said hello and Webster came in, hurriedly closing the door behind him. Then, with a sigh, he made heavily for an armchair and collapsed on it. He was sweating, his hair was ruffled and his collar was awry.

"What's wrong with you Bob?" the director asked.

"I'm besieged, I'm surrounded," the producer groaned. "Ever since I arrived a week ago, there's been this aristocratic old lady following me everywhere. She wants me to make a film about her family to help her get back the throne of a Grand Duchy I've never heard of." Bob fanned his face with his handkerchief. "And as if that wasn't enough there's a horde of little actors and actresses lying in wait for me and asking for a part in my next film. There are so many that if I hired all of them I could surely make the most colossal film of every time, something that would put a combined *Fall of the Roman Empire* and *Ben-Hur* in the shade."

"Why don't you make it then?" the director asked ironically.

"You're always joking you…" mumbled Bob. Then looking him straight in the eye, he added: "I could make a film like that if you agreed to direct it."

The director laughed. "Let's talk about something else then…"

The two men had a drink and started speaking seriously about their work. Gianni stayed and listened for a bit, but the talk was of things he could understand little: co-productions, contracts, distribution problems…

He picked up a couple of magazines and began leafing through them absentmindedly. Only then did he remember that there was the sea outside.

He went out on the terrace. The sun was high and dazzling.

Below him, beyond the trees and the street, there lay the yellow strip of beach, and beyond that opened out the glittering immensity of the sea.

Shielding his eyes with his hands, the boy made out the large coloured umbrellas, the wooden cabins, the people laying on the sand or swimming in the sea, and the sails passing by swiftly.

He felt happy and excited. After months spent elsewhere, he once again saw a beach flooded with sunshine, and a sea he could fling himself in among the leaping spray and foam.

He went back in and asked his father if he could go and have a swim.

"Good idea," the man replied. "What about it Bob? Shall we go too?"

"I can't," said the producer. "I'm under siege I tell you."

"We could get out by the service door and make a dash for it across the park."

"If you want to, let's have a try," Bob agreed, but he didn't sound convinced.

They went down to the ground floor, and after going through the kitchens, slipped out into the park. The trees cast still, deep shadows. It really seemed as if no one would catch them.

They turned down a little lane and made their way through the hedges and the flowering shrubs. They were sure they were out of danger when, right in the middle of the park, they heard someone calling in a shrill quavering voice:

"Mr Webster! Hello Mr Webster… wait, wait a minute!"

They looked round to see where the voice was coming from. Under a fretted ironwork pavilion, sitting on a wicker chair, there was a little old lady. She was wearing a white frock with a green flower-pattern on it, a little hat with a veil, and ankle-boots done up with a myriad of tiny buttons.

"Oh no…" groaned the producer as the little old lady get up and tripped quickly and daintily towards them.

"Is she one of your actresses?" the director asked, hiding a smile.

"If she was, nobody could play the terrible little granny better than her."

"Who is she then?"

"She's the aristocrat I was telling you about, the Grand Duchess Greta of Hapsburg. Ninety-five years old, cousin of the last sovereign but one of the Austro-Hungarian Empire, Francis Joseph. You'll hear about it now."

The old lady caught up with them, said hello, and then observing them through a lorgnette, began her narration.

"As I was telling you before, Mr Webster, it would be of prime importance to convince the Austrian government that, since the Archduke Albert would not marry Baroness Eleanor of Bamberg in 1837, the territories of Quirintia, Slavonia and Bucovina should have been left by the Hapsburgs to the younger branch of the Höenbergs. And the latter in turn would have united them with the territories of Carelia, Lower Posnania and Brombovia. Thus the collapse of the Austro-Hungarian Empire, which as you know took place in 1918, would not have swept away the Grand Duchy of Rutenia, to which I would now be the rightful heir. Mr Webster, don't

65

you think you could manage to convince the Austrian government of all this?"

"I'll do my best," said Bob with an eloquent glance over the top of his glasses at his friends.

"There would in fact be a sure way of convincing them," went on the old lady. "You just have to make a great film about the life of my great aunt Clotilde of Bavaria, who took part as a trumpeter in the siege of Sebastopol. Marie Clotilde is very important because it was she who persuaded the emperor Francis Joseph of the need to annex Bosnia and…"

"Grand Duchess, I'll have to go into this matter deeply," Bob interrupted her, brushing away the drops of sweat that had appeared on his forehead. He looked round in a daze as if seeking some impossible aid. Suddenly his face lit up. "Grand Duchess, look over here!" he exclaimed. "Do you see that tall proud-looking man in a magnificent uniform with lots of gold braid?"

The director, the boy and the old lady looked where Bob was pointing. The proud-looking man was the hotel doorman.

"Yes, I can see him," said the Grand Duchess, peering through her lorgnette.

"He's a very influential personage. He's no less than the Grand Chamberlain of the Principality of Brichtenstein. Explain everything to him, you'll see that he'll be all ears."

Bob didn't even give the old lady time to thank him for his invaluable advice. He bowed quickly, took his friend and the boy by the arm and made off at a trot.

"She's a dear old lady, really, very kind and quite harmless," he said as soon as they'd made their escape, "and I'm sorry to play a trick on her little hat. But I can't waste my time on any confounded Grand Duchy of Rutenia. I've got enough to do coping with these actors who are chasing me."

"I reckon this place is full of odd people," Gianni remarked.

"That's an understatement!" replied Bob. "At this time of the year the Venice Lido is a mecca for the maddest and most eccentric people in the world."

They were just coming out of the park when a noise above their heads caught their attention.

"There, what did I tell you?" Bob said calmly, pointing to a very high lime-tree. "Look up there."

Among the branches of the tree, perched at a giddy height, there were a man and five women.

The man had three or four cameras slung round his neck and was leaping from branch to branch as nimbly as a monkey, frantically taking photos of the five women. The latter, for their part, were continually putting themselves in different poses, each one more absurd than the other. But what was more absurd was the fact that none of them had fallen from the tree yet.

Listening to his father and Bob, Gianni learnt that the man was David Healey, the famous fashion photographer, and that the five acrobats were his favourite models.

"But why has he taken them up there?" Gianni asked. "Couldn't he take the photos on the grass?"

"On the grass there wouldn't be any originality in them," Bob explained to him. "Nowadays a fashion photographer wants to be different, he wants to pose his models in the strangest possible places. Well, Healey's a real master at this. Suppose there's a fire in a tyre factory. Haley turns up with his models and among all the smoke, the flames and the firemen, he does a tremendous series of photos that'll be published in some important magazine under a title like

Red and black will be next autumn's fashion. Another time, to give a fitting background to a collection of raincoats, he hired a small fishing-boat, loaded his five martyrs on it and sailed out into the North Sea in a storm."

"But what's he doing up there now?" Gianni asked.

"I suppose he's taking photos for an article entitled *Next spring we'll be all green.*"

Another reason for Healey's success, as Gianni heard later, was the tallness and the thinness of his models. The best-known one was called Tippy, stood six foot five and weighted eighty pounds. To keep her figure she slept only three hours a night and would eat nothing but flower-petals, preferably magnolia, orange-blossom and roses.

Gianni, his father and Bob left the cool shade of the park and walked down the avenue that led to the beach.

A colourful crowd on their way to and from the beach drew them into their gay, confused atmosphere. You could see the most unusual clothes and hear a variety of incomprehensible languages. The Film Festival and the bathing season had transformed the little island into an incredible open-air theatre.

They suddenly noticed a large group of people accompanied by a growing crowd of inquisitive passers-by. Gianni and the two men stopped to watch the strange group coming towards them. A moment later, when the crowd broke up a little, they could see what was happening.

A tall, beautiful woman, her head erect, was walking forward with a light step, holding a lead with seven blue-foxes on it. Her eyes were a golden-yellow, as were her lips and fingernails. Around her porcelain-like face hung long violet hair.

In front of the woman as if in a dance, her admirers were skipping and jostling, some offering her flowers, others holding out visiting-cards, and others begging her for a smile or an autograph. But the foxes, savage and cruel, drove the admirers back, snapping at the most daring ones, and opening up a wide path in front of their mistress.

Gianni recognized her at once. He had often seen her at the cinema or on television: it was Stella Dawn, the famous actress.

Stella came towards them, her eyes haughtily fixed on the horizon. She would certainly not have noticed them if Bob had not called out to her. Only then did she turn towards them, and when she recognized the director and the producer, she gave them a glowing smile.

They exchanged a few words, but as the crowd was collecting round them, they started walking on again together. Soon, preceded by the foxes, they moved onto the great beach.

Gianni couldn't wait to get in the water and rushed off to change. When he ran down the beach and dived in, the foxes, who had been left off the lead, followed him leaping over the first waves and plunging in around him.

For an instant Gianni felt afraid. It was only when he saw them splashing happily and heard them squealing with pleasure that he understood he had nothing to fear. Before a few minutes had passed, the boy and the foxes had started playing together like old friends.

Gianni stayed in the water a long time.

In the end tiredness got the better of him, so he came out and lay down to rest on the sand.

To while away the time he began to look around and amuse himself by picking out among the bathers the numerous characters who had come to make a show of themselves on the famous beach.

Not far from him, just where the waves finally gave up and retreated, there was the Caliph of Tuwait with his thin moustache, long satin caftan and giraffe-skin babouches.

Twenty retainers armed with scimitars were disposed around him, ensuring him a generous stretch of beach to himself. In the middle of this stretch, his platinum Cadillac with its mink seats was parked. When you raised up the lid of the boot, the latter was transformed in a grand-piano.

Now a Polish pianist, his long fair hair blowing in the wind, was playing at the keyboard of the boot.

With a flick of the hand, the Caliph ordered his thirty wives to move away from him; another gesture set them dancing. After this, he took off his babouches, lifted his caftan a little and, having stepped into the water up to his ankles, began very gingerly to paddle up and down.

The spectator's attention turned to another important character, who was just at that moment making his entrance on the beach.

It was the super-rich Maharajah of Bagore, known as "Green Smile" because of his set of emerald false teeth. The fat Maharajah, in a turban and a long silk garment, a small snakeskin whip fastened to his wrist, was half-lying half-sitting in a sumptuous sedan-chair that was supported by two small white elephants. When they came closer, Gianni saw that the Maharajah was engrossed in munching pieces of candied fruit one after the other from a large box.

When they were a few paces from the water's edge, the sedan-chair stopped, the fat man threw away the empty box and climbed out. At once, a swarm of pageboys gathered round him, holding a large umbrella over him and fanning him with peacocks feathers. As soon as he started lumbering towards the water, they began, with graceful movements, to throw pure-white lily-petals before his feet.

It was then that the Maharajah gave an icy glance at the nearby Caliph.

Gianni was amused to see that they were fierce rivals. The beach for them was nothing but a theatre where they could vie with each other in a display of luxury and riches.

Not far away there was a man who was indifferent to all this: the corpulent Luxembourg banker Jean-Claude Schlekenberg. Pink as a ham, continuously involved in producing puffs of blue smoke from his huge cigar, he had arrived just before, elegantly dressed in blue trousers and a triple-breasted jacket.

He had changed into an enormous pair of polka-dot shorts, and had made four employees carry his amphibious writing-desk and a huge computer into the water, together with a floating armchair on which he had sat and paddled himself a little way from the water's edge.

There he sat now, glad of the coolness of the sea, gently rocking with the waves. And there he had begun to work on the computer, studying and comparing the stock exchange quotations of the main weapons factories in the world. Every now and then he would pick up the receiver of one of the five telephones he had in front of him and sent mysterious messages to London, New York, Singapore, Hong Kong, Zurich, Shanghai...

Gianni had only had to turn his head to see some other protagonists of this great comedy of the beach.

Further on, hard to recognize but equally interesting, there was the modest, democratic King Gunnar of Norway and his family, who came on vacation to the beach of the Lido. They had arrived by bus, with a canvas bag from the depths of which had come sandwiches, bottles of lemonade and crossword puzzles.

For Gianni the rest of the day proved to be quiet and rather boring. His father was always busy talking about work with Bob and other colleagues who had arrived in the meantime.

Instead, the evening promised to be amusing because father and son were to go to a great reception that would be held in the villa of Gloria Simpson, the multi-millionaires actress, who in the Nineties had been the Queen of Hollywood.

At the end of the afternoon they all went back to the hotel. Thanks to a large straw hat he had bought on the beach and wore pulled down over his eyes, Bob managed to slip past the Grand Duchess Greta of Hapsburg and a swarm of little actresses without being noticed.

They had dinner, dressed smartly, and came out. It was the first time Gianni had been to a reception and naturally he felt very excited.

Chapter nine

Gloria Simpson's villa was literally besieged by a mass of sight-seers, photographers, autograph-hunters and ambitious young actors who, if it had not been for the surrounding wall and the sturdy gate, would have not thought twice about making a disastrous invasion. Their only aim, in fact, was at all costs to reach the glittering luxurious society that had gathered inside the villa.

The cars of the guests drove in slowly, passing through a narrow path in the midst of the crushing crowd. After a few minutes' wait the car with Gianni and his father also managed to reach the grounds of the villa.

The building itself, which must have been built in the early years of the twentieth century, was high and massive, decorated with stuccoes and flower patterns, with wrought-iron ornaments and stained-glass windows.

In the space in front of the villa, you could see a large floodlit swimming-pool, on whose surface thousands of tiny bubbles were continually bursting.

Gianni heard later that the pool was filled with real champagne. Some of the guests in swimming costumes were diving into the pool greedily and splashing around in cushions of pinkish froth.

Around the large pool, in the entrance of the villa and in the ground-floor ballroom, you could see countless guests in evening dress. There were film personalities from all over the world, industrialists and famous dress-designers.

Among the latter some stood out, such as Christian Doudou, with his large earring dangling from his right ear, his trousers held up by mink suspenders; Nina Mucci, the creator of the egg-style, who, naturally, was wearing a large plastic egg with only her head and her legs sticking out of it.

There were also members of the aristocracy such as Count Simeon Koroloff, accompanied by his haughty greyhound which wore a little black cloak. And of course, there was the sprightly Grand Duchess of Hapsburg, who, with her endless tales of great-aunts and principalities, had already driven half of a dozen guests to despair.

One of these who had tried to escape from her by gradually retreating while she was talking to him, had finished up by tumbling backwards into the swimming pool, raising a mountain of froth. Unfortunately he couldn't swim and when he managed to clamber out, a few minutes later, he was as drunk as a lord.

The flashes one after the other that lit up the villa's roof mystified no one: it was Healey the photographer, who had seized his chance to climb up there with his models and take a series of photos that some guests said would be called *Frocks on a moonlight night*.

Of course, the Maharajah of Bagore and his rival the Caliph of Tuwait were present.

To judge from the way they were eyeing each other, it would have been no surprise if at the drop of a hat they had started a furious duel with scimitars.

Stella Dawn, the actress, had got out of his car together with seven black foxes and had at once attracted the admiring glances of many of the gentlemen present, especially of the banker Shleckenberg, who, for the reception, was wearing a quadruple-breasted dinner jacket.

He had stealthily picked a dozen flowers from a flower-bed and had approached the lovely actress with the intention of offering them to her. The foxes, however, had obviously not found him of their liking - perhaps it was the cigar smoke - and had immediately barred his path with gleaming rows of sharp teeth.

The poor banker could do nothing but retreat to the buffet and console himself with *canapés of caviar*.

Gradually the guests gathered in the ballroom of the villa.

The interior was richly and fancifully furnished in the style typical of the time when the villa was built. Large pieces of furniture decorated with glass, with frond and flowers in dark metal, were ranged along the walls, upon which hung paintings and mirrors. There were also bunches of flowers, bronze statuettes, knick-knacks, ornamental plants and a gramophone with a large horn.

On the wall there was the portrait of a hunter in the African savannah. It was said that years ago an admirer of Gloria Simpson's, whom she had rejected, had fled to Africa in an attempt to forget his *femme fatale* by hunting lions.

Month after, the postman delivered a package to the star. Inside, she found a pair of boots, a cap and a rifle snapped at by the fangs of a big wild beast.

The guests were talking about this sad story when the butler, a dwarf in red livery, climbed up on a table and announced the arrival of the mistress of the house.

After this, he knocked on a table with a stick, and at once a large curtain opened. Behind it, on a dark wooden platform, there was an orchestra of harps, which at a sign from their conductor, began to play a languid English waltz.

Slowly, in time with the music, the fascinating Gloria Simpson, the star that would never set, descended the wide staircase with her person wrapped in a cloud of plumes, veils and jewels.

She greeted everybody with a wave of her hand, moved down among the guests, and the dancing began.

Gianni got a kick out of seeing the Caliph of Tuwait dancing with the egg-woman, the Maharajah hopping around propped up by his bodyguards, and the banker who, because of the foxes, could not get near enough to Stella Dawn to ask her for a dance.

An hour passed, and then another.

By now Gianni had seen all the possible variations of the spectacle, including a formidable slip which sent the Caliph belly-up in the middle of the dance floor, and a fierce struggle between the banker and the foxes. As a result, he began to feel bored.

Just to do something, he ate a sandwich of *hare pâté*. He still got a little fun out of watching the Maharajah of Bagore, who, after eating his way furiously through the buffet supper, gulped down two bottles of the famous wine *Mouton Rothschild 1973* as if it were water.

But after this, Gianni had to admit to himself that he was not only bored but also tired.

He went out into the villa grounds for a short walk. The night was cool and full of damp scents.

He walked along a lane until he saw that he had reached a boundary wall. There was a little iron door, closed by a bolt, and the curiosity got him to have a look outside to see if there was still anybody there. He opened the door and peeped out...

Suddenly a horde of fans and autograph-hunters who had long been waiting in the dark for a chance like this, charged in through the door.

It was the beginning of the end.

Gianni didn't even had the time to understand what was happening before an avalanche of people, exasperated by their long wait outside, swept into the villa grounds, shrieking with admiration, and in the midst of blinding flashes from a host of cameras, brandished notebooks and sheets of paper ready for the collection of signatures.

The storming of this crowd into the villa caused indescribable uproar.

The Maharajah of Bagore, afraid that a regiment of camel troops was charging in under the orders of the Caliph of Tuwait, commanded his men to draw their scimitars and attack his rival's bodyguards. In a split second, the rival troops closed in on one another with a furious clashing of blades. At once, half of the women in the room fainted.

With this the chaos was complete.

Careless of the dangers, in fact, spurred on by the sight of what was happening in the villa, the photographers rushed in, their blinding flash-bulbs going off wildly in all directions. The rest of the crowd followed, throwing themselves into the scrum.

The Caliph's and the Maharajah's followers threw aside their scimitars, which were useless in that bedlam, and came to grips in epic struggle.

Nobody knew and nobody will ever know how long chaos reigned there. Gianni came across his father, who had managed to get out, and together, from a safe space, they stayed to watch the incredible scene.

By the light of the photo flashes, which, through the stained-glass windows, looked like a firework display, people were scattering all over the house, were sliding down the drainpipes, rushing outdoors, being shoved out, going back in again, some through doors, others through the windows.

Little by little, the guests, who were trying to push their way out, got the better of the intruders, and the first effects of the cataclysm began to appear.

The Grand Duchess of Hapsburg came into view with the gramophone horn on her head. The poor banker ran out with three foxes swinging on the tails of his jacket. The Maharajah and the Caliph, locked together in a stranglehold, rolled down the steps. Bob came out with twenty-five actresses on his heels.

Gloria Simpson, the star that would never set, appeared looking like a gipsy who'd spent the night under a hedge. She ran to the garage, leapt into her fabulous yellow Duesenberg and roared off into the night.

The night's event had finally made her set.

Other guests tried to get away in their cars, but one of them, who was in too much of a hurry, skidded on the gravel and his car plunged into the swimming-pool. The splash that this made was so high it reached the tops of the trees and soaked and spattered everybody with champagne.

While the unlucky motorist was swimming to the edge of the pool, the others, refreshed by the shower, quickly calmed down.

The flash-bulbs stopped going off and the people grew silent.

The party was over.

Gianni and his father, tired and still bewildered, set out for their hotel.

"I wonder why a thing like that could have happened…" murmured his father.

"Well, hem… to tell the truth, it's partly my fault," Gianni timidly confessed.

The man gave a start. "What did you say?"

"Well, you see," the boy explained, "I was bored, and so…" Gianni quickly explained what had happened, and finished up: "Perhaps it's better if I stay on my own for the next few days, isn't it?"

"Yes, perhaps it is," said his father, ruffling the boy's hair.

They walked on in silence for a few minutes, then Gianni, out of the corner of his eye, saw his father was smiling, and asked him why.

"I was just thinking," his father said, "that in fact every cloud *does* have a silver lining. If you only knew how bored I was myself…"

Chapter ten

After leaving the great ship he had followed into the lagoon, Silverskin the dolphin swam towards the extraordinary city he had glimpsed so unexpectedly. He felt particularly attracted by a group of distant buildings that towered high, glowing above the water.

Over his head, suspended in the blue-green light of the sea, tugs, launces, ships and motorboats went by, trailing behind them a swirling cloud of tiny white bubbles.

When the fish of the lagoon saw the dolphin, they stopped, gasping in amazement. They had never been visited by such a large and lovely fish before. Some took fright and fled, but others worked up the courage, closed in and followed him, wondering where he was going.

Soon Silverskin found himself surrounded by a dazzling retinue of sardines, bass, soles, red mullets and cuttlefish.

Some of the fish came into a huddle for a minute or two, then a mullet plucked up courage and approaching the dolphin, swam alongside his mouth.

"Er... ahem... welcome to Venice..." he said rather embarrassed, turning even redder than he was already. "If you want to visit our city, I'll be glad to show you round."

"*Your* city?" said Silverskin in astonishment. "I never knew there was a city inhabited by fish..."

"Venice is," a sole said, swimming up close. "Normally we swim round the city's canals, but sometimes, when the tide is higher than usual, we can even take a turn round St Mark's Square, on the same spot where the tables are standing outside the bars at this moment."

"But who was it that built a city like this?" asked the dolphin. "We fish or men?"

"It's odd, but men built it," said the red mullet.

"Why did they do it? Men live on land, not in the water…"

"Well, there is a reason," the mullet went on. "Many centuries ago this place was completely deserted. There were just few fishermen and salt gatherers living here in poor straw huts built on the sandy little islands. On the mainland, however, only a few miles away there were rich prosperous Roman cities and towns."

The group of fish passed close to a long line of tugs and launches moored to the bank, one beside another. The water's glassy surface above their heads was getting busier and busier. They must have come near to the heart of Venice, now.

"One day," the mullet continued, "a terrible disaster struck the mainland towns. Hordes of barbarians, primitive peoples from the North and the distant lands of Asia, began to invade Italy, sacking and destroying everything in their path. The mainland towns were abandoned and the inhabitants fled to small isolated islands in the lagoon. The invaders, who had no ships, could not reach them there, and so they were safe. Venice was born at that time, more than a thousand five hundred years ago."

"I still haven't understood though," said the dolphin, "how the men managed to build such a big city on the water."

"Like this: they brought tree-trunks from the mainland, sharpened them at one end and stuck them into the muddy bottom of the lagoon. Then the trunks were joined tightly to one another so as to form massive platforms, called *palafitte*.

And then house were built using stones brought from the mainland in large boats. Slowly, as the centuries passed, a city grew up around those first houses, and the city spread out, becoming more and more beautiful. To build all the wooden platforms, the Venetians needed so much wood that they stripped some mountains in the Alps of all their trees. In time there came the Venetian conquest of the sea, the city's trade, its flourishing arts, industries, and the splendours of its sumptuous rich life. Where before there had been only water and strips of sandy earth, there rose, as if by miracle, the world's most powerful city, the richest in works of art."

Swimming and chattering, the fishes soon reached a group of marvellous buildings and monuments. They could see a great marble bridge, the Ducal Palace, the towering campanile of St Mark's, the two columns supporting the winged Lion and St Theodore...

Silverskin swam slowly towards the surface.

The statues and the stones of the buildings were veiled by the water at first, but as he rose higher and higher, he saw them more and more sharply, changing from sea-green to pale blue, and finally, when he broke the surface, they shone before him in all their dazzling whiteness.

At that very moment Silverskin heard his companions calling him excitedly: a launch was coming. He dived quickly and started swimming forward again.

A little later they turned into a luminous canal as wide as a large river and flanked on both sides by a view of fantastic palaces, churches and gardens.

"This is the *Canal Grande*," a bass told Silverskin, "the most important canal in Venice. It's about two miles and half long and runs right through the city, twisting and turning in a S-shape. Along its banks the rich and powerful Venetian families vied with one another in building the most beautiful palaces. Here at the entry to the canal they used to hang a thick chain across from one bank to the other to stop pirates from penetrating into the city."

"You've got some funny boats in Venice," remarked the dolphin, glancing up at a long slender boat that was just passing overhead.

It was black and curved at the bow and stern like a thin half-moon. At each end it had upright beak of shining metal, the one at the bow having six large teeth. There was a man standing in the stern and keeping the boat moving with a long oar.

"That's the typical Venetian boat and it's called *gondola*," the red mullet said. "It's twelve yards long, is flat-bottomed so that it can move in shallow water, and can carry six persons. These gondolas, which were been built more than twelve centuries ago, enjoyed periods of great splendour. In the Sixteenth century, for example, there were ten thousand of them, and they were finished off with gold and silver ornaments, rich cloths and cushions. During the winter the middle part of the gondola, where the passengers sat, was covered by a little cabin with small windows on it."

While his friends continued with their explanations, the dolphin, through the ripples of the canal's surface, was watching the incredible spectacle slowly unfolding above his head.

On the left appeared the *Basilica della Salute*, which was crowned by a majestic dome with statues and huge curls of white stone all round it. The fish told him that to build the Basilica more than a million tree-trunks had to be driven into the seabed.

On the canal's banks, Silverskin saw palaces of every shape and size, some tall and haughty, others delicate and almost weightless. Mosaics, statues, stained-glass, many-coloured arabesques and inlays made them look even more beautiful.

Between the buildings, canals and dark lanes wound their way into the city. In front of many palaces, thick wooden piles were sticking out of the water, painted with the typical spiral strips of colour.

The canal curved to the right and the fish passed the Mocenigo palace, where the famous English poet Byron lived in the Nineteenth century. He often used to swim the entire length of the Canal Grande.

They passed under the *Ponte di Rialto*, the bridge with a row of shops running across it on either side, and further ahead, against the bank, they saw a crowd of boats loaded with goods for the Rialto market.

Further on, glowing in the sunlight, there was the *Ca' d'Oro*, the House of Gold, the most famous palace on the Canal Grande. It had taken its name from the gold that once covered its façade. The dolphin could not help stopping to gaze at its decorations of coloured marble, its small lithe columns, its fretted balconies, and the diadem that crowned at its top.

"Along the Canal Grande they used to hold splendid fêtes," one of the fish began to tell the dolphin. "On summer evenings, endless processions of gondolas and other boats lit up by many-coloured Chinese lanterns would pass along it while the best singers competed with one another in singing serenades. To celebrate the arrival of important people in Venice, or when there were public holidays, magnificent spectacles were organized on the Great Canal. In 1541, for example, a number of barges were lashed together and an enormous construction was placed on them: it was shaped like a globe with the upper half cut off. Inside the half-globe, between its gorgeously decorated walls, two hundred ladies, as many gentlemen and an orchestra took their places. While the guests danced, and from the canal banks, the windows and the roofs a great crowd watched the spectacle, this fantastic construction was towed down the Canal."

By now the group of fishes had reached the end of the great waterway. They turned back, swam into a small canal on the right and thus penetrated into the labyrinth of the city.

"Yet the loveliest sight of the Canal Grande," went on the fish, "was and still is the Regatta. The origins of this event are very ancient, it goes back to the time when the bowmen of Venice used to go to the Lido once a week to practise with their crossbows. Their return from the Lido rowing in several boats always developed into a race. Thus in 1300 it was decided to hold a Regatta for the first time: it was to be a grand race among the gondoliers. The race was preceded by a procession of splendid boats including those called *peote* and *bissone*. The latter, for example, had eight oars and was decorated with statues, precious clothes, cushions and gilded stuccoes.

The oarsmen were dressed with similar magnificence. Besides providing a spectacle for the crowds thronging the banks, these boats also had the job of clearing traffic from the Canal Grande. The race was about to start and all hindrances had to be removed from the waterway.

At the front of the *bissona*, kneeling on a cushion, there was a nobleman with a small bow - he would shoot small balls of gilded clay at anybody still obstructing the way. Then amid the cheers of the excited crowd the gondolas in the race would arrive. They would row furiously the whole length of the canal, then, sweeping round a stake at the end, would come all the way back to reach the finishing line. The winner of the race received a red flag as a prize, the second a blue flag, the third a green one, and the fourth a yellow one together with a live piglet."

"Do they still hold the Regatta in Venice?" asked the dolphin.

"Yes, they do, once a year in September, as always," one of the sardines replied.

All the fish winked at one another, pleased at the news they had for Silverskin.

"You've been very lucky to turn up in Venice just now," went on the sardine. "The Regatta's being held tomorrow!"

"I'll be able to see it then, won't I?" the dolphin said.

When they told him he certainly would, he did a dozen of somersaults an pirouettes out of sheer joy.

The group of fish wandered around the maze of canals for a long time. Thus Silverskin was able to explore all the secret nooks and crannies of the city.

From time to time, muffled by the curtain of the water, they heard the short sharp warning cries of the gondoliers arriving at the curves and crossing of the canals. Twice in the course of the day they felt the water surging back and forth between the houses under the pressure of the tide. This current washed and refreshed the city.

Narrow and winding, the canals slowed down the ebb and flow of the water, preventing it from moving too impetuously. Only in this way had the city been able to stand up to the slow wear and tear of the tides for so many centuries.

Evening came and a sprinkling of moonlight glittered on the roofs, the bell-towers and the domes of Venice.

When the magical city was wrapped in sleep and silence, the dolphin enjoyed himself ploughing without restraint along the Canal Grande, dancing and hurling his gleaming body in the air, diving amid splashes of crystal water.

Chapter eleven

On the very same day, while Gianni and his father attended the party that Gloria Simpson had in her villa, and while the dolphin was wandering round Venice's canals, a brief storm had passed over the city.

The event didn't fail to have its effects on Alvin and the other dogs, who fled from the Rialto market after the clash with Cato the cat.

None of the small gang liked water very much, Alvin because of all the baths he had been forced to take, and the others dogs because they had too few. So when the clouds swelled and began to rumble, the dogs kept glancing anxiously at the sky. No sooner had the first large drops begun to fall than the whole gang took to their heels, scampering in all directions.

Each of them sought shelter on his own account, so that in a second or two the gang had broken up entirely.

Instead, Lord Peacock, his wife and Gea proved to be of sterner stuff as regards the rain: they were still walking round the quarter searching for Alvin. In spite of the first shower, they continued their hunt, unaware that the three thieves Rubino, Muscleton and Volauvent were dogging them.

On the other hand, the sausage giant, who had been following Muscleton, gave up straight away, not only because running wasn't his strong point, but also because after being robbed of a large sausage, getting soaked in a shower would have been the last straw.

A roll of thunder echoed round the sky. The rain started coming down in bucketfuls.

At that moment, Gea glimpsed in a side-lane a little reddish-haired dog who was just slipping through a door. The girl immediately called her parents and they all hurriedly made after the dog.

"It was one of Alvin's gang, I'm sure!" exclaimed Gea.

She was right. The dog she'd just glimpsed was Ali Baba, one of the most active participants in the day's turmoil. Having lost sight of his companions when the first drops of rain fell, he'd dashed straight back home.

"I don't see what use this dog is to us, though," remarked Lord Peacock. "I hope, Matilda, you don't want to take him to replace Alvin."

"Edward, be serious for a moment, can't you?" she urged. "That dog is a clue, a precious clue that may help us to trace Alvin. That's why we'd better follow him."

The three of them went into a small entrance and up some stairs. The dog was standing in front of a door.

"What do we do now?" Matilda asked.

They began to consider the painful question, staring blankly at Ali Baba.

When he'd seen the strangers stopping behind him, Ali Baba had felt rather uneasy. And when he realized they were staring at him, he began to scratch at the door desperately.

At last the door opened and a man appeared.

He had long unkempt hair and there were a lot of little coloured stains on his shirt, trousers and hands. From these signs, together with the smell of oil paint coming through the open doorway, the three of them gathered that he was a painter.

"Ahem... er..." stuttered Lord Edward, just to start a conversation that promised to be very difficult.

"Ah, it's you!" the painter exclaimed happily. "Very pleased to meet you! Come in, your pictures are ready..."

"Oh... but perhaps..." Edward said, having expected anything but a welcome like this.

Then, since the man was insisting on them going in, they did as he wanted.

"I hope you didn't get wet just coming here," the painter remarked.

"Oh, no," Matilda assured him with an embarrassed smile.

Edward would have liked to explain at once that there had been some mistake, that he hadn't come to collect any pictures, but his attention was so violently caught buy what he saw around him that he just stood there gaping, as did his wife and daughter.

The walls, doors, furniture and ceilings, everything in fact, was painted in bright colours. You could see enormous figures of insects, machines, women and tigers. There were tubes of paints all over the place, canvases heaped one upon the other, bundles of drawings perched on the furniture, stuffed owls and crocodiles, a large branch of a tree hanging on the wall, antique guns, manikins, bicycle wheels, a mountain of torn posters, and any number of other incredible objects.

In a corner, there was also the painter's son. He had dug a trench between the canvases and was playing cowboys and Indians by himself.

"Come on, Mr Martin, come and see the pictures I've got ready for you," their host said, taking Edwards by the harm and guiding him to a corner of the studio. Matilda and Gea followed.

The paintings were imaginative, full of life and colour, but you couldn't understand clearly what they represented. And this, for Edward, was rather a serious fault.

"Very nice," he said, "but, you see… ahem… the fact is that I'm not Mr Martin."

"You're… you're not…" stammered the painter.

"No, I'm not."

The man passed his fingers through his hair ruffling it up even more. "Oh, I'm sorry," he said. "I've been expecting Mr Martin to come for some days now and since I've never met him…" He fell silent, gazing out the window at the boats passing on the Canal Grande. "Mr Martin had written saying he would come and buy my pictures."

Edward felt himself blushing with shame: what could he tell the man now? That they'd come to the house in search of a dog that had been together with their dog and other dogs too?

"But there's only this dog here," the painter would have answered.

And then Edward would have to say: *"Yes, but this dog is a clue."*

"A clue to what?"

"A clue to find our dog."

"I assure you your dog is not in the house."

"Yes, I know…"

"Well, what do you think you're doing, looking for him here?"

"Heavens, what a mess…" thought Edward.

No, it was really out of the question to let oneself in for such a stupid conversation. And then, disappointing the poor painter like that…

A light but eloquent nudge from his wife elbow brought him back to earth.

"Well… that is," he said, "even though I'm not Mr Martin, I intend to buy your pictures all the same."

"Do you really?" the painter exclaimed. "You already know my work, then?"

90

"Oh… hmm…" burbled Edward. A meaning nudge from his wife brought his voice back. "Yes, of course I do. I've seen your paintings in several exhibitions."

The painter, his happiness now complete, decided to offer his guests a drink. In a wardrobe he found a couple of bottles mixed up with withered flowers, wire and a lifebelt. Then he took the glasses out of a drawer. The corkscrew was in the fridge together with the washing and some books.

They drank, chattered about art, and eventually the artist offered to paint Matilda's portrait. She and her husband protested, but the offer was repeated so sincerely and convincingly that in the end they had to accept.

The painter went to another room to get his brushes.

"And what do we do now?" Edward hissed at Matilda.

"Keep an eye on the dog. If he goes out, follow him."

"Ah yes, wonderful! And how can I explain that to the painter?"

"Think of something," whispered Matilda, as their host came back.

The painter got Matilda to pose for him, opened the door of a wardrobe and began to paint on the inside of the door.

"I haven't got any canvas left," he explained quite naturally. "But you have no difficulty in carrying the door away with you."

Soon after, the storm having passed, the dog went to the door and started whining. He'd had just about enough of those strange characters. And the fact that his master had made friends with them didn't affect him a bit.

"Mr Peacock, would you mind opening the door for him please?" asked the painter, not wanting to leave his work at the most difficult moment.

Edward gave a start. "Oh yes, of course," he said, and getting up went over the door. "Ahem... I think I might go out too. I wouldn't mind a stroll..."

He called Gea and asked her if she'd like to come, but at the moment she was too busy. Together with the artist's son she was painting blue and yellow stripes on a stuffed crocodile.

As Ali Baba was going down the stairs, he noticed that the strange character was following him. A cold shiver ran along the dog's spine: so his suspicion had been right, these people really had it in with him! A family of dog-catchers, perhaps?

Edward and the dog came out into the lane and walking on, reached a square.

The sun, having torn aside the thick leaden clouds, was now shining in the puddles and on the dripping marble. The air was limpid and fresh-smelling.

The unlucky Ali Baba looked around for his friends. Nobody in sight.

Damn, only if the gang had been there, he wouldn't have been afraid of this character. Anything but! He would have shown his teeth in a snarl, and even got a grip on his trousers just to teach him a lesson.

But now, all on his own...

He tried running, and the man started running too. He slowed down, so did the man. There was no doubt about it: he must be a dog-catcher. Perhaps, the chief dog-catcher.

Ali Baba suddenly caught sight of a tavern. It was open and full of people. He had an idea: if he went in there and stayed crouching in a corner, the dog-catcher could never get him in the middle of all those people...

The next moment Edward saw the dog dive into the bar and slip under the tables. Quickening his pace, he went in too.

The tavern was crowded and noisy. The tables had been put together to male two long rows, and the people sitting there were having a really good time. They were laughing, drinking and singing to an accordion. Many had glowing cheeks and eyes.

At the centre of the rows of tables, in the shadow, there was the gleam of a white dress.

Edward was intent on peering under the tables to see where the dog had got to, when he thought he heard someone speaking to him.

He looked up and saw that in fact one of the wedding party was, with broad gestures, inviting him to sit down at table.

Lord Peacock smiled and shook his head politely, but the other man insisted, calling on his friends for help.

"Come on boys, you tell him to come and join the party!" and he pointed at the new arrival.

A chorus of voices was raised, which weakened Edward's resistance. And a burst of cheering and clapping finally did the trick: he gave in and took his place between a gondolier and a carpenter. In front of him there was a large flask of red wine.

They filled the glass for him, and then another. Edward drank and soon felt like talking.

"My name is Edward," he said to the gondolier.

The gondolier shook his hand as only a gondolier knows how. "My name is Tony" he replied.

"I can see you've finished eating," he said to the gondolier. "but I wonder if it's possible to… you see, I haven't eaten anything so far today."

The gondolier looked at him in disbelief: a man so well-to-do, elegant, with a trim moustache and clean fingernails, forced to skip meals?

Lord Edward understood the question in the man's eyes. "Oh no, my friend, it's not what you're thinking!" he exclaimed with a laugh, slapping the man on the back. "I've not eaten because… well, because of my dog. Funny, isn't it?"

Tony stared at him astonished. "You let the dog eat your dinner?"

"No, no. It's just that the dog ran away and we had to chase him. I've been running after him all day."

The gondolier gave it up. "Well, now I'll get you fixed up," he said, and called out some orders to the kitchen.

A few minutes later Edward saw arrayed before him a soup-dish, plates and trays loaded with gorgeous food.

He ate and drank his fill.

The longer he stayed there, the gladder he was at having fallen in with such cheerful and hospitable people.

He joined in the singing, made a short speech, and then, with the accordion accompanying them, danced with the cook's wife.

When at a certain moment Tony suggested a trial of strength, Edward was the first to agree.

The tables were cleared and the tournament began. In couples the diners faced each other, trying to force the opponent's arm flat on the table. Whoever lost was eliminated.

Edward did much better than he'd expected. He beat the bridegroom, two waiters, a fishmonger and, only just, the cook's wife, so that he finished up eighteenth best. The overall winner, of course was Ironarm the gondolier.

To celebrate the end of this epic struggle, another regiment of flasks was put on the tables and the singing was taken up again.

At this point, while the party is still going on, we might leave the cheerful tavern for a moment to take a look outside at the little sun-drenched square.

Sittings on the steps of a building, and worn out by hours of waiting, we find Rubino and Muscleton.

When Edward left the painter's house on the track of the dog, the two thieves had followed him. Instead, Volauvent had stayed behind to keep a check on Lady Peacock and her daughter.

Muscleton suddenly got up from the steps and suggested Rubino should do the same. "I've had enough," he said decisively. "I'm tired of waiting. And I haven't eaten since last night."

"What do you want to do?" Rubino asked him.

"Let's go inside and let's see what he's up to!"

"All right, maybe it's better that way," his companion muttered. "He might even have slipped out the way back…"

They went into the tavern and began to scrutinize the diner's faces one by one. Lord Peacock was there, his cheeks as red as ripe apples, and his glass raised up in yet another toast.

The two of them turned to go, but a chorus of voices, even louder than the one that had greeted Edward two or three hours before, halted them at the door.

The diners' enthusiasm in this case was not only due to them wanting to make the party bigger: the looser in the trial of strength contest had in fact market down the giant in the tight jacket and the overshot trousers as a champion who could even beat Tony, the victorious gondolier.

Rubino pretended not to hear and dodged out of the door. Instead Muscleton, who had smelt the intoxicating perfumes coming from the kitchen, hesitated a second.

That second was fatal.

Suddenly, without knowing how it happened, he found himself sitting at a table, a great napkin tied round his neck, and a fork and a spoon clutched in his hand. Rubino had to resign himself to come back inside and sitting down the table.

Muscleton's meal was a grandiose event, an episode that in centuries less arid than ours would have provide inspiration for the most famous artists. He ate everything the cook and his wife offered to him: from a huge pot of spaghetti to a gigantic rib eye with baked potatoes, from a double dish of clams to three slices of wedding cake. The whole thing washed down with a flask of red. Then he started again with a casserole of shrimps, two loaves with a block of cheese, and, finally, a whole watermelon.

When they saw what was happening, the other guests stopped singing, and sat down around him, completely dumbfounded. Someone went into the square and called the passers-by to come and have a look. Soon half the district was packed in front of the tavern door and window.

In the end, when the tavern's cellars and kitchen were exhausted and Muscleton had had his fill, a new trial of strength tournament started amidst much laughing and shouting.

Naturally, Muscleton outdid his rivals with the greatest of ease. During the contest, however, some nasty things happened to him.

In the first trial his right sleeve burst open. In the second, the back of his jacket ripped to pieces as did his collar and the left leg of his trousers. In the third trial most of all his remaining clothes fell apart and he was left, as usual, in a striped t-shirt and flower-pattern pants

Despite this, he got carried away by the contest and didn't worry overmuch about what was happened. He was so enthusiastic in fact that when had to battle it out with Lord Peacock he didn't take very much notice of him.

Muscleton's feats in the contest equalled those he had achieved at table. He defeated two, three and five men together. Not even ten of them could force his arm onto the table.

For his part, Edward did even better in the second tournament than the first: he beat two barbers, the bride's uncle, a fisherman, and Rubino.

Yes, Rubino.

However, the fumes of the wine were sure to make both of them forget this strange meeting.

It was already evening when the party broke up.

They all came out singing. Muscleton had a flask of wine in one hand and a table-cloth tied round his waist. After they'd all said goodbye to one another, each staggered off home.

Volauvent had been hiding in front of the painter's house all this time and was still on his feet thanks only to his exceptional willpower. When he saw Rubino and Muscleton supporting each other and tottering towards him, he thought he was dreaming.

From the way the two of them were gaping around, it was obvious that they'd never managed by themselves to find the spot they'd started out from, so Volauvent went forward to meet them.

"You oafs, what have you been up to?" he whispered hoarsely, waving a threatening forefinger at them. "Where have you been? And what on earth are you wearing, Muscleton?"

"Something comfortable at l… hic! … last," stammered the giant. "But why didn't you … hic! … didn't you come? You would have… hic! … enjoyed yourself."

"Oh, yes... en... hic! ... enjoyed yourself!" echoed Rubino. Volauvent's face turned as red as his companions'. "Where's Peacock?" he hissed.

"Peacock? Hic!... I've heard that name somewhere before..." muttered Muscleton.

At that moment, Volauvent's attention was attracted by the sound of teetering footsteps: it was Lord Peacock coming back. Volauvent grabbed hold of Rubino and Muscleton by the arm and dragged them into hiding.

Edward took some time to find the painter's house. When he got there at last the moon was high in the sky.

Matilda, of course, greeted him rather coldly, but he didn't take it amiss. The afternoon in the tavern had given him a fund of good humour that would last him at least fortnight.

He examined his wife's portrait with curiosity: it had been finished during the day.

"Very very interesting... hip! really," mumbled Edward. "I'm just trying to under... hip! to understand if I'm blind drunk, and as a consequence I can't see... hip! where the heck Matilda's eyes are finished, or if the painter forgot to depi... hic! to-do-de... depict her eyes..."

The painter watched Lord Peacock thoughtfully for a few moments. "I see that you have read my mind," he said. " I painted Lady Matilda without her eyes as a symbol of the human existence. She *can't see* a meaning in our pursuit of happiness..."

"You're right," agreed Edward. "In fact... hic! we spent the whole day in pursuit of our beloved dog Alvin..."

"Edward, for heaven's sake!" implored Matilda. "Our friend prepared the beds for us. Why don't you set a good example?"

"What do you mean?"

"I mean: why don't you get a good night's sleep?" asked Matilda. "Gea is already sleeping."

"Wonder... hic! Wo-wonderful idea, darling" stammered Lord Peacock.

Chapter twelve

After hearing the Lion's stories, the flock of pigeons took off from St Mark's Square and flew towards the inner part of the city.

Among them was Phoebus, who, as he gradually discovered the beauties of Venice and got used to the peaceful, almost unreal rhythm of life there, was growing more and more convinced that it was the very place for him.

For a while they flew over houses and canals, then over a square dominated by the solid bulk of a large church, and finally arrived over another little square.

Here, in front of an imposing church and a small palace with a rich marble façade, there stood a bronze statue of a warrior on horseback.

"Look, that's Bartolomeo Colleoni," one of the pigeons told Phoebus, pointing the statue. "He was a great *condottiero*, the bravest Captain General Venice has ever had."

"While the Republic's fleet was always put under a Venetian," explained another pigeon, "command of the army was, by tradition, handed over to an outsider. Colleoni, in fact, was born near Bergamo, a town at five days on horseback from Venice."

The birds flew down towards the monument and with a swift fluttering of wings perched on the helmet and the shoulders of the warrior.

Colleoni was sitting erect on his saddle, his legs fully extended in his stirrups. A proud frown was stamped on his face. His mouth had a haughty expression, and his eyes stared without wavering at the horizon.

He was holding the reins in his left hand and with the other he grasped a commander's baton.

Phoebus bent down to his friend's ear. "Psst... listen," he whispered. "What's he so sulky about?"

"I'll ask him to tell you, if you like," his friend replied, speaking in a normal voice.

"No, no, for goodness' sake," hissed Phoebus. "He'd only get even angrier..."

"Don't worry, he's only very kind to us pigeons. If he didn't have us to chat with now and then, he'd have to sit here in silence all the time, alone on his pedestal..." The pigeon turned to the warrior: "Mr Colleoni, our new friend would like to know why you look so sulky."

The statue looked down at Phoebus, staring at him with such steely eyes that the poor pigeon felt the blood freeze in his veins. He was just going to fly away when unexpectedly the trace of a smile crossed Colleoni's face.

"You're right, it's true, I'm a misery," he said, raising his helmet peak, which had been casting a shadow over his face. "But I have my reason for always being in a bad temper, by the blast of thousand cannons!" he exclaimed, waving his baton in the air. "I'm a fighting man, I'd always lived in the din of a battle and ridden at the head of great armies... And just look at the miserable state I'm in now. Instead of the clash and thunder of a battle, I'm forced to listen to the housewives who stop for a chat under my pedestal. Instead of soldiers in shining armour, I'm surrounded by strange individuals wearing coloured shirts and dark glasses. They come here in droves, stare at me as if I were something out of a zoo, and point weird metal contraptions at me..."

"They're tourists," a pigeon explained.

"*Tourists*?" repeated Colleoni, as if the word was Arabic. "What does that mean?"

"People who come and visit Venice."

"And what do they do exactly?"

"Well, they see everything there is to see, churches, palaces, islands, canals…"

"Thunder and lightning! In my time we'd have arrested 'em all as spies! And now instead… ah, what times these are for heaven's sake!"

"Oh, come on, Mr Captain, don't lose your temper," a pigeon said soothingly. "After all," he went on, "Venice isn't at war with anyone anymore…"

"You can never tell," insisted Colleoni. Then, lowering his voice: "The dukes of Milan and the lords of Florence could be plotting in the dark…"

"Don't worry," a pigeon perched on his helmet reassured him. "If anything happens, we'll make sure you get due warning."

"Speaking of spies…" said Colleoni, in a suspicious way, "there is a certain white dove who comes here every day and perches on my helmet. I don't like her."

"Why, Mr Captain General?" asked a pigeon.

"She is cheeky, and she always says those strange, unpleasant things to me…"

"What kind of things?"

"Remarks about war and peace…"

"What does she say, exactly?"

"She scolds me saying that I'm a nasty man for having led so many wars! Just think that Venice dedicated a monument to me, for this reason!"

"And what else does she say?"

" It's incredible: she tells me that I should make peace with all my enemies! I think that she must have been sent to spy on me by the Duke of Milan!"

The pigeons smiled. "No, no, Mr Captain, take it easy," said one of them, "we know her. It's Emma, an ordinary Venetian white dove. She's harmless, believe us."

"Well, all right, she isn't a spy, nevertheless she's a big nuisance!" thundered Colleoni. "A few days ago she perched on my helmet, as usual, and immediately started telling me that I should be ashamed of my military misdeeds, and that I should stop sitting here playing the role of the war hero!" Colleoni was furious. "And to top it all off," he added, "she even pecked my nose! It was an outrage against the history of Venice!"

"Yes, you're right, Mr Colleoni," one of the pigeons tried to calm him down, "actually Emma is a little shrewish, but deep down she's really a nice girl. She's just a member of the pacifist movement."

Colleoni widened his eyes. "Pacifist movement?" he yelled. "What the devil is that?"

"It's a group that supports the ideal of peace and love all over the world, and…"

The Captain General interrupted the pigeon. "I'll never ever make peace and love with the Duke of Milan!"

"No one wants to force you to get along with the Duke of Milan," said the pigeon. "On the other hand, Emma is obviously a pacifist."

Colleoni, frowning, gazed at the pigeon. "Why obviously?"

"Because the white dove is an international symbol of peace," replied the pigeon. "You understand Emma couldn't help becoming a pacifist…"

The Captain shook his head. He was puzzled.

"Hmmph…" he grumbled.

The pigeons scanned Colleoni's face in silence.

"All right, then, but tell Emma not to peck my nose again," sentenced the Captain General.

All of a sudden, however, he burst out again.

"I'm a warrior, by Jove!" he shouted. "For a man like me, used to riding at full gallop, it's no joke being stuck up here like a dummy! If this pedestal wasn't so high, I swear I'd jump down and make off! But you'll see, one day or other I'll come to the end of my tether and do just that."

"Don't you like Venice?" Phoebus asked him.

"Well, yes, I like it. Even if…"

"Even if?" the pigeons asked in chorus, craning their necks towards him.

"Even if the Venetians played a dirty trick on me, by the blast of ten thousand bombs!" the Captain General roared, striking his great fist on the bronze saddle.

The pigeons, gave a start and drew their neck back.

"What… what trick did they play to you?" said Phoebus in a frightened whisper.

"Humph… well, I'll tell you then. In my times, in the Fifteenth century, Venice was fighting a terrible war against the Turks. I wanted to help Venice, so in my will I left the city a hundred thousand gold pieces. But I left them at one condition: that they should… ahem… in fact, they should put my monument in St Mark's Square, in front of the Basilica. After all, I deserved it, with the victories I'd won for them!"

"And instead…"

"Instead the government of Venice decided that no man, not even I, was worthy of such a great honour. So as you see, they put my monument here, in front of the church of St John and Paul. It's not the same thing, shattering thunderbolts!"

"Cheer up, Mr Colleoni, you know this square is reckoned to be the loveliest in Venice, after St Mark's. And just look at the monument they've made you. Haven't you heard that yours is the most beautiful equestrian's statue in the world?"

"Hmmm… that's as may be," muttered Colleoni. On his face, now, there was not only indignations, but also a hint of pride…

"And what about the honours the Venetians gave you for each of your victories? And the rewards you got when, for the first time in history, you put wheels on cannons?"

"By Mars, what times they were…" Colleoni exclaimed. "I remember the day, it was the 24th of May 1458, when I came to Venice to be proclaimed Captain General. I, the officers under me, and two hundred knights, had travelled to the shore of the mainland. In front of us, on the water, there were already more than a thousand ships and boats waiting for our arrival, and soon after the Doge himself arrived in a magnificent gilded galley. They brought me to Venice and in the Basilica of St Mark's. There, with the most sumptuous ceremony I had ever seen, they handed me the commander's baton. And I remember the celebrations held in my honour on the following days, and the tournaments, in which the bravest knights vied with each other…"

As he thought back to his proud, distant life, Colleoni gradually calmed down.

It wasn't easy for the pigeons to get him to cheer up. And now they succeeded, they didn't want to spoil it.

The pigeon on the helmet brought the tip of his wing to his beak so to hush his companions, and silently took to the air.

A moment later the others followed, passed over the houses around the square and flew off.

The flock returned to St Mark's Square, where Phoebus was introduced to the statues one by one.

On the Clock Tower he met the Two Moors, black and strong, who beat a bell with long hammers every quarter of an hour.

Then he met St Mark, who was standing on the top of the diadem that crowned his Basilica, and all the angels, shining white with golden wings, poised on both sides of the saint.

Lower down, on a terrace jutting out from the Basilica façade, there were four great horses in gilder copper: they were carved in Greece four hundred years before Christ, afterwards they were taken to Rome, and from there, centuries later, they went to Constantinople, where they were set up at the entrance to the Hippodrome on high pedestals.

One of the pigeons explained to Phoebus that in 1204 Constantinople was conquered by the Crusaders, and the Venetians brought these horses to their city. When, in 1798, the French marched into Venice, Napoleon saw the horses and had them moved to Paris together with the Lion.

Finally, in 1815, they were brought back to Venice and have stayed here ever since.

The birds moved on to the Ducal Palace, on which you could see the majestic statue of Justice.

She was clutching a huge sword in one hand and with another was holding up a pair of scales. On one tray of the scales some young pigeons were perching and enjoying themselves by see-sawing up and down.

The new arrivals were just flying away when Justice nodded at Phoebus, who stayed behind.

"You've not been in Venice long," she said to him, "so I want to give you a piece of advice. Look down there at the corner of St Mark's Basilica, close to the ground: can you see those four statues?"

Phoebus picked out the point she'd indicated. Against the wall of the church, there were two couples of warriors in porphyry: they were pitch-black and each couple was locked in each other's arm.

"Beware of them," the statue said sternly.

"But... but who are they?"

"An ancient legend tells they are the Four Moors, the Saracen thieves who came to Venice to steal the Treasure of St Mark's. They managed to get into the room where the Treasure was kept and carry it away with them, but when the time came for them to share it out among themselves, they quarrelled, drew their sword and killed one another. Thus the Treasure was recovered, and now stands in its place in St Mark's Basilica."

The story made a great impression on Phoebus, who stood there rooted to the spot, staring at the four statues.

But his friends were in a hurry. They came back, calling his name, and persuaded him to fly off with them.

The flock gained height quickly and when they were well above the square, headed for St Mark's campanile, which towered above the other buildings.

On its top, about 330 feet above the ground, there was an enormous gilded angel with outstretched wings. He was standing on a revolving platform, and the wind, whistling through his wings, made him turn slowly and face continually in a different direction.

The birds settled on his head, wings and arms.

Phoebus looked around him. From up there, the view was tremendous.

"This is the Archangel Gabriel," a pigeon told him. "As he stands higher than any other character in the whole of

Venice, he's been able to see and learn a lot of interesting things. Just listen a bit."

The pigeon said hello to the angel, introduced Phoebus, then asked if he could tell them some of his stories.

"I'd be glad to," the great statue was prompt to answer, since, being so high, he rarely had any visitors. "This time I could tell you about the most attractive of Venice's celebrations, or to be exact *The Feast of Carnival Thursday*. Indeed that day was an unforgettable experience for everybody.

In the square down below, before the Doge, who came out on the balcony of the Ducal Palace, and in front of the nobles, the magnates and all the people of Venice, a marvellous spectacle was staged. It began with the *Flight of the Turk*, a display which was called this because of something that happened about the middle of the Sixteenth century. A Turkish acrobat anchored a boat in the water off St Mark's square and strung a rope from the boat to the top of this campanile. After this, he walked all the way up the rope, keeping his balance just with the aid of a wooden pole.

Every year after that, many Venetians repeated this dangerous feat. The *Flight of the Turk*, however, which was performed during the Carnival, was a little different. The rope was stretched from the top of the campanile to the balcony of the Ducal Palace, and a winged young man who was attached to the rope by rings, flew down it, coming to a halt just in front of the Doge. He presented the Doge with flowers and a scroll of parchment which had a poem written on it. After accepting the gift, the Prince of Venice gave him a bag of money as a reward, then the young man went back to the top of the campanile, where he gave a display of acrobatics.

During the *Carnival Thursday* of 1680 an incredible thing happened. There were no stairs inside the campanile, but a soft ramp where people could go up walking. In certain occasions eminent figures, like the Doge, climbed the tower on horseback. "

The wind, which at that height was rather strong, blew in gusts against the Archangel's wings. The great statue turned slowly, stopping only when it faced in the direction of the sea. "During the celebration of that Carnival," the Archangel started again to tell, "a boatman named Santo had the permission to ride his own horse up to the bell-room and from there, climbing up the sheer smooth walls, he scrambled up as far as the pedestal I'm standing on. When I saw him, I couldn't believe my eyes. But that wasn't all. In absolute silence, with the whole city gaping up at him, he then clambered along my golden robes onto my shoulders, and then onto my head, just where I wear my diadem. Well, do you know what he did once he was on top?"

The pigeons, without moving a feather, their eyes fixed on the Archangel, didn't reply.

"He took out a fan and cooled himself off, had a good drink from a flask of wine and finished up by waving a flag. The next year, on the same day, Santo climbed up to me again and balanced on my diadem standing on his hands and head and waving his legs in the air."

The Archangel waited for the wind to turn him round again towards the square. Then, pointing to the Doge's Palace, he went on. "When the *Flight of the Turk* were finished together with the other displays, a group of ten men, standing down there, in front of the Doge's balcony, performed acrobatics called *The Labours of Hercules*. Here's how they were done: some men climbed up on the other's shoulders, layer after layer, till the formation reached a remarkable height. They represented in this way some very telling scenes and compositions by changing the shape of the formation. For example they made scenes representing *The Colossus of Rhodes, Beautiful Venice, The Four Angels,* and *Glory.*

Sometimes *The Labours of Hercules* were performed in a barge on the water - this was less dangerous but more difficult, of course, because of the rocking of the waves. After these entertainments, the spectators saw the *Moresca,* which was a fencing match performed by many men, but in a dance rhythm and with blunt-edged swords. And then, to finish off the show, there was the Firework Machine."

"The Firework Machine?" queried the pigeons.

"Yes. It was a splendid construction, made mainly of wood, plaster and other light materials. It was high, very elegant and richly decorated. It had three storeys, each with its own orchestra. Scattered all over its surface there were thousands of rockets, crackers and Catherine-wheels. When the fuses were lit, it took only an instant for the Machine to be transformed into a little volcano, a cascade of thousands colours. What a sight it was, my friends!"

The Archangel turned towards the distant mainland. The sun was setting, dipping itself in a tangle of fiery clouds.

Beneath them, it looked as if all the reflections of a gigantic bonfire were playing on the city roofs, the marble of the palaces and the mosaics.

"I'd like to tell you another story," the Archangel said, "the last one before you go. On 25th August 1609 this campanile was visited by a crowd of very important people, who came up to the bell-room. At their head there was Galileo Galilei, one of the greatest scientists in history - at the time he was teaching in the Republic of Venice. Beside him was the Doge Leonardo Donato, and they were followed by a long line of senators and gentlemen. Galileo was carrying a leaden tube about three feet long and covered by red satin.

When they reached the bell-room, just under here, he put the tube on wooden support, pointed towards the sea and said to the Doge: «I have the honour of presenting your Serene Highness with a new invention of mine, the *Cannon of Long Sight*, an instrument of great scientific and military importance. With this you can see a ship at sea two hours before it is visible to the naked eye. If you, please, put your eye to the end of the tube and look through it.»

The Doge looked through the telescope - since it was in fact a telescope - and uttered a cry of astonishment: what Galileo had told him was true. "For hours and hours that day all the most powerful people in Venice climbed up to the bell-room and saw for themselves the extraordinary instrument Galileo had invented.

The Senate wanted to reward the scientist and so they doubled his salary. Thus thanks to the intelligence of the Venetian senators, Galileo was able to perfect his instrument and begin the exploration of the heavens."

The Archangel had finished his story.

The pigeons stood watching the sun, which was slowly being hidden by the clouds. Then they opened their wings and fluttered down to their resting places for the night.

Chapter thirteen

After the chaos he had unintentionally caused in Gloria Simpson's villa, Gianni, you'll remember, had decided to spend the rest of the holiday on his own at the Venice Lido.

As soon as he got up next morning, he started to think about what he should do. He went through all the different possibilities, and finally thought he would spend his time doing some underwater fishing.

In a shop he hired flippers, mask, harpoon gun and oxygen containers, and then went to a long quay that stretched out into the sea.

Here, after undressing and putting on his equipment, he dived in.

The water was clear, almost colourless. The boy swam on slowly, looking around. Thick shoals of fish brushed past him as they slipped away, others appeared among the seaweed. Large lobsters crawled suspiciously on the sea-bottom, waving their antennae.

At this point the sea wasn't deep. Gianni saw a slope covered with fluttering plants gliding past beneath him and then the sand, white and rolling, reappeared.

He swam on for a while. Suddenly, where the sea got darker opening out on the abyss, Gianni caught sight of a large fish. He brought his gun forward and darted towards it.

The fish didn't seem to have noticed him. Gianni swam and swam as fast as he could go, but despite of all his efforts he could not lessen the gap between him and his prey. This chase lasted a long time, and the more Gianni saw he was getting nowhere, the more he wanted to catch up with that strange fish.

Eventually, almost without realizing what had happened, he found he was a long way from the shore.

It was then that the fish put on a burst of speed and rapidly disappeared. There was nothing for Gianni to do but stop and curse his bad luck.

He was already turning to go back when he glimpsed an astonishing vision that stopped him dead in his tracks.

From the darkness of the sea there had appeared, and now was rushing towards him, a group of fantastic beings.

On a chariot drawn by wild sea-horses he made out a giant of a man, clutching a trident in one hand and the reins in the other.

Round his head he had a thick shock of green seaweed which was being whipped back by the speed of the chariot's rush. His face was partly covered by a long beard, also of seaweed. At his side, strange sinuous creatures, half-men and half-fish, were swimming together with marvellous-looking girls whose skin was the colour of the sea.

The giant pulled on the reins. The sea-horses reared up, making the water swirl around them, and came to a halt panting, their nostrils dilated, not far from the boy.

At that moment the fish Gianni had been chasing reappeared. The fish went up to the giant and told him just three words.

"It's him."

The green-haired man stared at the boy with terrible eyes. "So you wanted to kill one of the fish of my retinue!" he roared. His voice was deep and hard.

"No… no…" Gianni stammered out. "I didn't know the fish was yours…"

"So, why do you want to kill fishes? Maybe you need doing that because you're hungry?"

"Eh… no," replied the boy. "It's… it's a kind of sport…"

" Well, you don't need to kill fishes" the giant, said, speaking in a strangely calm tone of voice. "Yet you wanted to kill them with that kind of arrow…"

"To tell the truth, I just *tried* to do that," Gianni said in whispers.

"You wanted to kill a living creature, and you did it just to play sports!" the giant shouted . "Can you see that?"

"Yes…" Gianni said. "Yes Sir, I can,"

"Then, if you don't need to kill fishes, don't kill them!" shouted the giant. "They are living creatures, and you can't kill them

"Yes Sir, I swear I won't do it again."

"Throw that gun away!"

When the boy had obeyed the order, the giant added quietly: "This time I'll overlook it. But… watch out. Don't you ever let me catch you hunting my fishes again."

"I'll never do it again," Gianni hastened to say.

"Do you know your way back from here?"

"I think so."

"We're quite a long way out, you know," the giant said. "Maybe the current has taken you right out."

"I hadn't noticed…" Gianni said, looking round anxiously.

"Well… after all, I've taken a liking on you," the giant grumbled roughly. "Come up here, I'll take you back."

The boy swam between the sea-horses, which pawed the ground nervously as he passed, and climbed into the chariot.

While Gianni watched him out of the corner of his eye, the giant shook the reins lightly. The horses obediently moved forward.

They passed through a short stretch of sea, then the boy decided to speak. His curiosity was stronger than his fear.

114

"But you… who are you?" he asked the towering man.

"I'm Neptune, worshipped by the ancients as the God of the Sea. The waves, the currents, and all the sea creatures obey me. Look at this trident."

Gianni looked.

"If I beat the waves with it, powerful storms arise. But a gesture from me his enough to make the waters calm again."

The boy pointed to the strange creatures swimming round the chariot. "And who are they?"

"Those beings, half-men half-fishes, are Tritons. You see the horn made from a conch that each of them is carrying?"

"Yes," the boy replied.

The giant made a gesture to the Tritons. Immediately they lifted the conchs to their lips and blew with all their might. The result was a deafening booming sound like the crash of waves in a storm.

"It's those creatures with the horns that make the waves roar," Neptune explained. "As for the girls swimming alongside them, they are the Nereids, the nymphs of the sea. Their movements and the colour of their skins are exactly the same as the waves'."

Gianni was fascinated as he watched the fantastic creatures gliding along beside the chariot. At that moment his glance happened to fall on the reins that Neptune was driving the sea-horses with.

They were of gold and ware made up of numerous rings joined one to the other. Every time the giants shook these long chains, the sunlight coming from high above made them gleam rich yellow.

"I see you're staring at my reins," Neptune remarked. "Do you know what they're made of?"

Gianni shook his head.

"They're made of rings that belonged to the Doges of Venice."

"To the Doges? How did you get them then?"

"It's a very old story. Do you want to hear it?"

Gianni's timidity had vanished. "Yes please," he said decisively.

"Well, about a thousand years ago the Venetians beat all their enemies and became the masters of the Adriatic Sea. To celebrate their victory they began to celebrate a solemn ceremony, which they used to perform every year."

As Neptune was talking, he grew less and less gruff, until he sounded quite friendly.

"So," he went on, "it was during these grand ceremonies that for over seven centuries I enjoyed myself collecting Doge's rings and putting them together to make these chains."

"Collecting the rings?" the boy asked. "But... how could you?"

"I'd like to tell you, but look over there: we've almost arrived."

Gianni saw the giant was right. The sea-bottom was sloping upwards, the quay he had entered the sea from had appeared in the distance - a dark shadow in the clear water.

"Oh what a nuisance!" the boy grumbled. "I was enjoying the ride so much... Listen, Mr Neptune, couldn't you just tell me the story of the rings?"

The giant was thoughtful for a moment, then, with a jerk of the reins, he made the sea-horses turn in a wide sweep until they were heading for the open sea again.

"All right, I'll tell you the story of the rings, while I'm giving you another ride. Satisfied?"

"Yes, I am!"

The giant took up his story again.

"The ceremony I was telling you about was called *The Marriage of the Sea*. The Doge, accompanied by all the most important people in Venice, used to leave the Ducal Palace in his ceremonial robes, and at St Mark's quay he would embark on the Bucentaur, a large and superb galley propelled by oars. I know all the seas in the world and I've seen all the ships that sail them, but few of them could rival the beauty of the Doge's galley. The Bucentaur was gilded all over, and was decorated with statues, velvet and precious inlays. At the bow, above two great spurs that jutted forward, there was a majestic statue representing Justice, and at the stern there was a statue of Victory. On its only mast fluttered a huge five-tailed standard bearing the image of the Lion of St Mark's."

"How many people could the Bucentaur carry?" Gianni asked.

"Nearly four hundred. There were a hundred and sixty oarsmen, four to each oar sitting in rows on the vessel's lower deck. The rest of the crew consisted of a hundred sailors. On the upper deck, which had a great red velvet canopy over it, there was room for the Doge himself, the city's nobles, senators, priests, ambassadors, famous visitors and the three admirals who commanded the vessel. The Doge sat in the stern on a throne embellished by statues of Prudence and Strength."

While Neptune had been talking, the Tritons and Nereids had come closer and closer. Even the sea-horses had slowed down so that they could hear better.

"The Bucentaur's departure was saluted by the ringing of all the bells in Venice and the booming of the artillery. The crowd packed along the shore broke into defending cheers. As the vessel was passing, you could hear the songs of the oarsmen and see the waters tinged with a rainbow of reflections - and on these reflections hovered a swarm of smaller vessels among which there were magnificent gilded gondolas with canopies over them.

"And the rings?" asked Gianni.

"Well, the Bucentaur used to reach the island of the Lido and from there it moved out into the open sea, coming to a stop more or less above the place where we are now. Then the Doge, clasping a gold ring, would face the sea. When all around him had become silent, he would say in a solemn voice: «We marry thee sea, in sign of true and perpetual dominion». Then, the Doge would throw the ring into the sea. The Tritons and the Nereids were waiting: as soon as they saw the ring dropping through the water, they would grasp it and bring it to me. That was how, year after year, I collected the rings that make up these reins."

The boy stretched out his hand and touched the thin chain with the tip of his fingers.

"Would you like to drive my chariot?" Neptune asked.

"You bet I would!"

"Have a try then," and the giant handed him the reins.

Gianni took them, but he must have tugged them because the sea-horses pulled up with a jerk in a flurry of currents.

"Hold them very very loosely," Neptune suggested.

Gianni obeyed, and the sea-horses moved off again, but quietly this time.

The Master of the Seas let him drive for a while, then he took the reins again and turned the chariots towards the lane.

"You must go back now," he said to the boy.

The latter, who didn't have the slightest wish to return to the Lido, got sulky. And to make his intentions clear, sat down in a corner of the chariot.

"Come on, be reasonable," Neptune urged. "You're a boy, not a fish."

Gianni shrugged: "If I go back there, I'm sure to be bored to death."

Neptune fell silent for a while.

"I'll let you drive my chariot again," said the giant. "But only on one condition. That we go back to the Lido."

"Hmmm..."

"Besides, I'll tell you a story..." "

Chapter fourteen

The dawn of a new day spread over the sky of Venice.

The painter's house was plunged in silence. The Peacocks were sleeping soundly amidst the piles of paintings, the rocking chairs and the stuffed crocodile. Tired out by all their rushing the day before, they would certainly have slept till noon if nothing had happened to wake them.

But fate decided their rest was not to last so long. No sooner had the sun gilded the roofs of the city than a small gang of dogs started barking under the painter's windows.

Lady Matilda was the first to emerge painfully from her deep sleep. She was floating in the mist between sleeping and waking, when she gradually began to distinguish a well-known bark, a familiar voice, among the yapping of the others…

"Alvin!" she suddenly cried, jerking upright in the bed and looking round her.

Ali Baba, the painter's dog, was at the window, listening to the calls for him that were coming up from the street.

"What are you doing up there, come down!" a dog barked.

"There's the Regatta today, don't you remember?" another added.

Then you could hear Alvin's voice, which Lady Matilda would have recognized among a thousand: "Get a move on, or we'll go without you!" Matilda leapt out of the bed. "Edward! Gea!" she cried. "Wake up! Alvin is here!".

The woman threw open the door and rushed down the stairs.

Ali Baba tumbled after her, overtook her, and reached the street a second or so in the lead.

"Alvin!" Matilda shouted again, holding out her arms towards her beloved dog.

Her appearance and the desperate cry she let out threw the dogs into confusion. Like a shot they all turned tail and with Ali Baba at their heels scampered headlong down the deserted lanes.

The woman was on the point of following when it abruptly occurred to her to see that she was wearing a nightdress and had no shoes on. There was nothing for her to do but charge upstairs again to Edward, who was still sleeping snugly with an angelic smile on his face.

Gea was already standing. "Mum, what's happening?" she asked.

"Alvin is back!" she replied. "Edward, quick, wake up!" she cried, shaking him impatiently. Then, seeing he had simply turned over, she whipped off the blanket. "There's Alvin outside! Get up, we must go at once!"

Woken by the hullabaloo, and told of what had happened, Edward had to give up his bed.

Of course, when they reached the street, Alvin's gang had vanished.

The man looked around with sleepy eyes. "Well, what's the next move?" he asked. Then, since there was no answer forthcoming: "All right, if you don't mind, I'm going back to bed," he added, and made for the door.

Matilda's voice rang out in the silence of the early morning like the crack of a whip: "Edward, come back here, please!"

When Matilda sounded like that, it was no use arguing.

Edward smoothed down his ruffled hair, did his collar up, buttoned his jacket and retraced his steps. "Here I am my dear, at your disposal," he said.

While this was happening, an equally lively scene was taking place in a large fishing boat moored to the bank of a nearby canal.

Volauvent, Rubino and Muscleton, who were sleeping in the boat, had been wakened by the yapping of the dogs and Matilda's shouts, and had dashed to a small hatch to see what was going on.

After taking a look, they knew they had to get out as quickly as possible and threw on their clothes in a mad rush. In the confusion, Muscleton managed to get his legs tangled up in a fishing net, and Rubino put on Volauvent's jacket. But in the end they groped their way out, cursing that confounded dog, and hurried off on the tracks of the Peacocks.

The chase, however, didn't last long. When the Peacocks realized that Alvin must by now be far away, they soon slowed up.

Around them, little by little, Venice was waking up.

The women, who had started their housework, leaned out to chat to one another from the windows. The workers, early-risers who had to go farther than the others to their work, came out of their houses. And after opening their shops, the shopkeepers swept their piece of pavement or stood at the door enjoying a breath of the fresh morning air.

Up above, the amethyst sky echoed more and more with the chirping of the swallows.

Edward, Matilda and Gea arrived to a small square, sat down at the table outside a bar and had breakfast. On the canal in front of them, from time to time, the dark sleeping water was stirred into ripples by the first boats of the day.

The black outline of a gondola appeared.

All of a sudden Edward put down the cup he was holding, got up and reached the bank of the canal. He wasn't mistaken: the gondolier was Tony, the winner of the strength contest in the tavern, the day before!

"Tony!" he called. "Hey, Tony!" he called again, this time shouting. The man in the gondola stopped rowing and looked back, towards him.

"Edward!" he cried. "I never expected to see you!" He rowed back and quickly came up to the side of the canal. "What are you doing up at this hour?"

"We're still looking for our dog. And you?"

"I'm working. It's a great day today."

"Why?"

"It's Regatta day. All Venice will be on the Canal Grande."

"Are you in the Regatta?"

"No. I'm just taking tourists to see it."

Edward had at once an idea. "What about taking us to see the Regatta?" Edward asked Tony.

"I'd like nothing better!" the man exclaimed. "But it'll be quite a time before the Regatta starts, you know…"

"That's all to the good, I'll be able to rest a bit. I'm tired of galloping up and down the streets of Venice. Hold on a minute, I'll go and get my wife and daughter."

Gea was enthusiastic about the idea of taking a gondola, but Matilda didn't appreciate it.

"First of all I would like to know how it is that you're on first name terms with gondoliers," she said, and to underline the question started drumming her fingers on the table.

"Well, you know, I'm not familiar with *all* the gondoliers," Edward corrected her. "This is a friend of mine. If you really want to know, I met him yesterday afternoon in the tavern. And he won the first trial of strength contest."

"Very interesting," commented Matilda, looking the other way.

"Please dear, let's go in the gondola."

"Yes, mum, how could we come to Venice without going for a gondola ride?" asked Gea.

"All right, suppose I agree to the presence of that... hmm... *friend* of yours. And Alvin? What about Alvin?"

"We can carry on the search in a gondola," Edward reassured her. "In fact it will be easier to find him this way and won't wear us out."

Reluctantly Matilda got up and followed her husband and Gea.

Tony was very polite to her. He called her «Milady», helped her very carefully to step down into the gondola, and set her down on the best cushion.

Then the boat only had to move away from the moss-covered side of the canal and begin gliding nimbly over the water for Lady Matilda's mood to change completely. Like Edward and Gea, she had to abandon herself to a feeling of wonder and admiration.

Seen from down there, Venice looked lovelier than ever. It was as if the city had suddenly shown them a new face, more genuine and fascinating than the others.

Everything was extraordinary: the antique gates at the entrances to the houses with the water lapping gently against them; the gesture with which Tony bent down to pass under the lowest bridges; the trees that spilled over the walls of mysterious gardens, closing out the sky overhead and turning the canals into green tunnels; the washing hanging out to dry on clothes-lines stretched from one wall to another of the houses; and above all the silence, the absolute silence that reigned in the loneliest canals.

While our friends were entering this enchanting world, the three thieves were engaged in heated argument.

When, shortly before, the Peacocks had got into the gondola and sailed away, the trio had tried to follow them on foot. Then, finding it was impossible, they started searching desperately for another gondola to continue the pursuit, but at that moment there wasn't the ghost of a gondola in sight.

What were they to do?

"I give up," said Muscleton, and sat down at one of the tables outside the bar where the Peacocks had had breakfast.

He was on the point of ordering an extra-large cup of cappuccino, butter galore and fourteen brad-rolls, when Volauvent took him delicately for an ear and made him get up, saying to him sternly: "But *I*, my friend, I'm not giving up!"

Rubino expressed his opinion: "After all, I don't think Muscleton's really wrong. We've been running after the Peacocks for three days now, and all we've got is sore feet and a heap of trouble."

"But it's a matter of principle, of our professional dignity, don't you see?" exclaimed Volauvent. "What kind of gang are we, if a runaway dog is enough to make nonsense of all our plans?"

"Ahem… you're right there," muttered Rubino.

"It's essential for us to follow those three until they go to their hotel," Volauvent insisted. "When we get our hands on milady's jewels, you'll see that I'm right."

"All right then, let's get on with chasing them," sighed Muscleton with a resigned air. "But how? Do you want us to swim, by any chance?"

"And don't forget that Muscleton can't go around like that," pointed out Rubino, with an eye on the big man's striped tee-shirt and the table-cloth round his waist.

"Ah yes, that was all we needed," snarled Volauvent. "Was it really necessary to get mixed up in stupid games in a tavern? You didn't give a thought to the suit you were wearing, did you?"

"No, I didn't," the accused man confessed, looking down at the ground. "I get carried away, you know…"

Volauvent was too bad-tempered to restrain himself from quarrelling. "Have you looked at yourself in the mirror?" he went on angrily. "You look like… like a Turkish bath attendant!"

Volauvent was really furious. He would surely have read the riot act to Muscleton if Rubino hadn't suddenly interrupted and brought him back to earth.

"Hey, come and have a look at this, quickly!" Rubino was on the canal bank pointing at something underneath him.

His friends joined him. Moored at the piles there was a large empty boat.

"You think you can chase them in this monster?" asked Volauvent.

"Seeing there's nothing better…"

Volauvent raised his right eyebrow. "Why don't we use a transatlantic liner?"

Muscleton leaned over the side, looking wistfully at the large boat. "I could steer it, if you like…" he said.

They had no choice, as Volauvent had to admit.

They lowered themselves stealthily onto to the boat deck and undid the mooring ropes. Muscleton went to the rudder, while Rubino tinkered for a while below deck until a muffled roar announced that the motor had started. Slowly the boat slipped forward.

For a few minutes they had no difficulty in following the way the Peacocks had gone, but soon they came to a crossing of three canals. It was here that their troubles began.

They chose the right-hand canal, but in turning Muscleton misjudged the distance. The boat took too wide a curve, collided with the bow of a gondola and send the gondolier flying into the water.

Muscleton was highly amused. He turned to watch the unfortunate gondolier's efforts to get back on board his boat.

But, as often happens, fate was ready for its revenge, the arrow already drawn back in its bow. Muscleton didn't see that the large boat was steering crooked, did not hear the cries of warning of his companions. They hit the side of an another boat moored to the canal bank, and the recoil knocked the three of them off their feet. Rubino finished up in the water, and Volauvent tumbled into the other boat, which was full of black grapes.

Panting and puffing, the two men clambered back on board, Rubino dripping wet, Volauvent dyed a deep purple. While they were trying to dry themselves and get cleaned up in some way or another, Rubino suddenly stopped, white-faced.

"Hey, where's Muscleton?" he asked, his voice hoarse with emotion.

They looked around: there was no sign of him.

"Good grief!" Volauvent exclaimed, kneeling down on the edge of the boat and peering at the water.

Rubino seized a boathook and, his face screwed up with sorry, began frantically to sound the bottom of the canal.

They had just decided to throw the boathook aside and dive into the water, when Muscleton's voice spoke calmly from just behind them:

"What are you up to? Have you lost something?"

They sprang round. Muscleton's carroty-red hair and beaming face were sticking up out of an open hatch.

So that's where he got to, the fulltime fathead! He'd fallen in the hold!

Rubino boathook flashed out the water, described an arc in the air and thudded on the hatch. If Muscleton hadn't ducked with lightning speed, there would have been a clash between his head and the boathook, with serious consequences - above all for the boathook, since by all accounts Muscleton's head is harder than wood.

They set off again, this time with Rubino at the rudder. But the incident had brought the trio's morale very low.

Volauvent looked as he had just crept out of a barrel of wine. Muscleton, who was skulking crestfallen in a corner, didn't dare to glance at his companions. As for Rubino, with tears in his eyes he had watched his elegant yellow-striped blue suit slowly shrink with the canal water until it was incredibly small. All at once Muscleton's voice rang out again.

"Look over here!" He stood up and pointed towards another smaller canal. "Isn't that the Peacocks' gondola?"

Rubino and Volauvent stared. Good grief, *it was*!

At the rudder, Rubino swung the boat round abruptly and they entered the narrow canal. All three of them were so intent on watching the gondola that they didn't see what was happening.

The canal got narrower and narrower. The sides of their boat were almost scraping against the canal banks until...

When they did notice, it was too late. With a squeaking and crunching that set their teeth on edge, the boat jammed between the walls of two houses and came to a dead stop.

Rubino got the motor running at full speed forward then backward over and over again. The only result was a lot of noise and swirling water.

"That's really fixed us," he said, his forehead bathed in sweat.

Muscleton took the boathook and tried to push off from the canal bottom. Volauvent helped by shoving with his hands against the canal side. It was useless, the boat was stuck fast.

Defeated, they turned the motor off and sat down on the deck. All they could do now was wait for another boat to come along - "If possible, not a police launch," commented Rubino.

A while later, Volauvent was gazing at one end of the canal when he saw a gondola appear with the figure of the gondolier balanced on it. With a sigh of relief the three prisoners rose to their feet, waving to attract the gondolier's attention. But a closer look told them there was no cause to feel light-hearted.

The gondolier now speeding up to them, in fact, was the one Muscleton had sent flying in the canal shortly before. And behind him, as reinforcement, there was a small fleet of other boats.

They looked round searching for escape. The walls towering above them were smooth and high, without windows. There was just one opening in the wall at their height, but it was behind a heavy gate.

Volauvent went and had a look at it. Behind the gate there was a damp slippery flight of steps that led up into darkness.

"Muscleton!" he called out with decision. "It's up to you."

With a couple of leaps the big man reached the gate. The need to regain the prestige he had lost with his companions, and above all his fright at what was happening, gave him ten times the normal strength - which was already remarkable.

He grasped two bars, flexed his biceps until they stood out like rugby balls, and with a powerful twist wrenched the gate from the wall.

The steps lead to a wooden door which Rubino opened in a second with one of his picklocks. They went in, shut the door and looked round.

They were in a large room which had great wardrobes lined up all round its walls. Dusty beams of sunlight filtered through some small windows up near the ceiling.

Their professional instinct lead the trio directly to the wardrobes. They opened them and rummaged inside…

"Just look at this! It's great!" Muscleton mumbled happily, pulling out a musketeer's costume complete with long sword, plumed hat and cloak.

They had apparently finished up in a theatrical costume warehouse.

"Let's find something we can put on, and then get out of here," whispered Rubino, taking out a circus ringmaster's outfit. "What about this, would it be all right? Leaving aside the top hat, the whip and the boots, of course."

"And the jacket with tails?" remarked Volauvent. "You can't go out with that…"

They began sorting through the wardrobes again, till they found what they wanted. Volauvent put on a naval captain's uniform, Rubino found a butler's livery and Muscleton…

"But where is Muscleton?" asked Rubino. "Muscleton, don't play the fool, come out here!"

A screen opened and the big man danced out dressed as an Arabian sheik. "At last I've found something comfortable!" he exclaimed enthusiastically. "These are the clothes for me!"

Volauvent, unfortunately, didn't agree. "Get those sheets off at once!" he commanded.

The smile of joy vanished from Muscleton's face. He went back behind the screen, rummaged through a wardrobe again and came out a minute later wearing a pair of ballet-dancer's tights and hopping about on the tips of his toes.

There would certainly have been a fight between him and his friends, if at that moment they hadn't heard shouts of alarm and the sound of footsteps rushing along upstairs…

"Someone's coming!" hissed Rubino. "Maybe it's the gondolier! Quick, let's move!"

He and Volauvent opened a door, found a corridor and dived down on it. At the end, under the light coming from a semi-circular window, there was a heavy wooden gate. They opened it and found themselves in the bright daylight of a square.

People stared when they dashed out dressed like that. Little boys started jeering.

Rubino and Volauvent didn't waste any time. With a tremendous sprint they got clear of the crowd. Only when they'd gone a good way, did they realize that Muscleton wasn't with them.

"He must have stayed behind in the warehouse," murmured Rubino. "When he get enthusiastic, he can't think straight anymore."

They walked on in silence, looking at the ground.

"They'll have got him by now," Volauvent said.

Rubino shook his head sadly. "It's fate. It had to happen sooner or later."

Now, deprived of Muscleton and having definitely lost tracks of the Peacocks, they had to admit that their trip to Venice was a complete failure.

They would stay there a little longer, but only as tourists. And just to relax a bit, they'd go to the Lido beach. Before finally leaving, when everything had quietened down, they'd find out what had happened to Muscleton.

As they talked on these things, the pair of them reached the foot of the Rialto bridge. The vaporetto to take them to the Lido was just coming in. They broke into a run to catch it, but at that moment Volauvent glimpsed at the top of the bridge's steps something that made him pull up with a jerk.

That sly, elusive dog of the Peacocks was there, together with his gang.

An idea flashed through their minds: if they could catch the dog, they could take him back to the Peacocks, get friendly with them, and perhaps accompany them back to their hotel...

After exchanging a brief but eloquent glance, the two of them went into action. Volauvent stopped at the bottom of the bridge, while Rubino crept up the steps, crossed the top without the dog seeing him and slipped down to the other side.

A whistle from Rubino and operations began.

Very slowly they began to saunter up the steps from opposite ends of the bridge, gazing unconcernedly at the Canal Grande. Each watched the dog out of the corner of his eye.

They came within a few steps of him.

Alvin was playing with the other dogs and took no notice of the men. He only saw what was happening when they were already almost on the top of him.

On one side he glimpsed a naval captain, blue uniform and brass buttons. On the other, a small dark-haired butler. They were crouching down, arms outstretched, ready to grab him.

He retreated slowly, snarling, while the two men got closer and closer…

A lightning glance between the columns of the parapet told him that a big cargo boat was just approaching under the bridge. As his persecutors dived at him and their hands touched his fur, Alvin jumped off the bridge.

The void opened beneath him, and he fell twisting in the air, his legs kicking out, flying without breath, while the world somersaulted around him - water houses sky people merging in one endless round of giddiness.

Luck was with him. He plummeted right in the centre of the boat, in the midst of rolls of cloths, velvet drapes, gilded tassels and fringes.

Alvin didn't know, but the cloth in the boat were for the finishing touches to the boats that were to take part in the forthcoming Regatta.

He felt slightly dazed for a moment, then, coming to himself, he looked up towards the bridge. The strange characters that had tried to catch him were up there, leaning over the parapet and gazing at him incredulously.

After a short trip the cloths boat reached a vast, covered mooring place where numerous, splendid art boats for the parade were lined up.

Alvin, however, had no time to admire them because people were coming, and he had to get away quickly. Jumping from one boat to another, he finally took shelter in a small gondola.

He stayed there a long time. Every now and then he poked his head out to see whether he could make his escape. But every time he had to draw it in again quickly because there were scores of people coming and going, hurrying to get the boats ready.

All of a sudden Alvin heard footsteps approaching.

He hid again, trying to make himself as small as possible. At that moment the gondola quivered under the new weight of two men. Then he heard the rhythmic splash of two oars in the water. A moment later they were out in the dazzling sunlight.

As happened every year, the Historical Regatta had begun.

A happy, stately procession of boats made its way forward, entering the Canal Grande, whose banks were thronged with people. Among all the other boats, the slender, elegant *bissone* stood out. They were painted in bright colours, and embellished with gilded and silvered statues, coats-of-arms, flags and canopies.

At the side of each *bissona*, dipping and rising in a regular rhythm like thin wings, you could see eight oars painted with white and red or white and blue stripes. The rowers, one to each oar, wore colourful costumes.

When the long procession had passed, everybody looked towards the end of the canal. From down there the nine small gondolas in the race would soon appear.

Little by little, the wind along the great waterway brought the spectators the sound of distant voices, cheers and applause like the advancing tide. A few moments more, and a roar of approval went up from the waiting crowd. The gondolas had come into sight, and were moving swiftly, swinging forward in a confused rash blur of arms and oars.

Alvin, who till then had been lying flat on the bottom of one of the racing gondolas, began to get really worried.

Who were all these people yelling around him? And why were they yelling? Were they after his blood?

As the din grew louder and louder, the dog brooded anxiously over such questions till he couldn't stand being hidden there a second longer. He plucked up courage and darted out, ready to plunge into the water as soon as anybody tried to catch him.

What he saw came as a great surprise to Alvin, as great as the spectator's astonishment when they caught sight of him. The two oarsmen in his gondola were so struck by his popping out that they slackened their efforts and were at once overtaken by all their rivals.

Instantly from one of the many gondolas crammed with spectators at the canal side, there rose a cry:

"Alvin! Stop him, stop him!"

It was Lady Matilda of course. Together with Lord Edward and Gea on Tony's gondola, she had been engrossed in the race.

Flushed with emotion, she turned to Tony. "Quick, Tony, follow him! Follow him, please!"

"But... Milady, I can't..." the gondolier replied. "It's forbidden!"

"Hurry, or he'll get away again!" she insisted.

Losing his patience, Edward chimed in. "Tony, a thousand pounds for you if you help us to get that dog back once for all!"

The gondolier hesitated for a moment. Then the generous offer made for him. He pushed the gondola out fast, dipped his oar in the water and started rowing with all his might.

The chase lasted for a good stretch of the Canal Grande, amid the amused cheers and shouts of the crowd.

The crew of the racing gondola, who had slowed up when Alvin appeared, now went even slower when they saw themselves pursued by the Peacocks' gondola. What surprised them the most was the sight of Lady Matilda standing upright in the bow like a pirate ready for boarding.

135

The two boats were now quite close and were about to touch when an extraordinary thing happened.

Without the racing gondola's crew making the slightest extra effort, their boat suddenly whipped ahead and started ploughing through the canal water like a streak of lightning. In its irresistible course it overtook all the other competitors, and amid mad cheering from the crowd crossed the finishing line with a hundred yards to spare.

Naturally nobody could explain this mysterious turn of events, least of all the crew of the racing gondola. But since there was no reason to believe there was any trick or irregularity involved, the jury decided to award the winner's flag to the two dumbfounded oarsmen.

After all, everybody eventually agreed that the little dog must have been a remarkable good luck mascot.

It's clear, though, that this explanation is by no means satisfactory. In fact we'd better make an investigation on our own account to find out what lies beneath the surface of this affair.

Let's leave the sounds and colours of the Regatta for a while and, as the Peacocks' gondola is nearing the jury's stand, dive below the waves of the Canal Grande.

Here, in the green silence, we find an animal we've met before: Silverskin the dolphin, who got back again into the scene of our story. From underwater, swimming to and fro, he had followed the different stages of the Regatta, and had got excited like all the other spectators when the race was nearing to the end.

When, however, he had seen a small black and white dog appear on one of the racing gondolas, and another gondola had dashed out from the canal side, and a woman in the bow had waved threateningly at the dog: when, at last, the two boats had almost touched…

No, by Neptune's beard, he, Silverskin the dolphin, would never allow anyone to be harmed, not even that strange little animal!

Swiftly he reached the threatened gondola, eased his back under the boat's flat bottom and then, with a powerful sprint, tore it away from the threat of being boarded, and carried it unawares to victory. Having done this and seen that the dog had been picked up and was now safe, he had gone off waggling his fins in satisfaction.

Observing the scene, in the middle of thousands of people who had flocked to the banks of Canal Grande, there were also two chaps who we know only too well: Rubino and Volauvent. They had decided to stop following the Peacocks and their dog, but when they saw that little hated dog aboard a racing boat, and behind him the Peacock dashing in pursuit, they felt convinced they should remain there and not give up the struggle. What was taking place under their eyes was a challenge of fate, a challenge they would be ashamed to refuse.

They ran towards the finishing line, shoving their way through the crowd so roughly that more than one spectator risked falling in the canal, and got there just in time to see another astonishing incident.

The Peacocks had climbed hastily onto the jury stand and dashed towards Alvin. But the dog, although he was being stroked and patted by a hundred different hands, although he was having his whiskers pulled and, in fact, his breath taken away, managed all the same to sense his master's approach. And, as he hadn't yet made up his mind about returning under Lady Matilda's secure but suffocating wings, he had gone into action.

A decisive snarl, a wicked-sounding bark, and the host of enveloping hands instantly withdrew.

The gap they left was enough to him to take a run-up, twist and turn his way through the legs of the by-standers, shoot along the bank and finally disappear down a lane.

The Peacocks had spent hours relaxing in the gondola - Edward had even had a nap - and now felt on the top of their form, so they set off in hot pursuit, followed by Rubino and Volauvent.

The Venice merry-go-round was still whizzing round, faster and funnier than ever.

But let's go back to the sea in front of the Lido' beach. There, Neptune, the Sea God, had promised to Gianni he would tell him a story.

Chapter fifteen

"What kind of story will you tell me?" Gianni asked Neptune.

"Let me think about it..."replied the god. "Maybe... maybe I could tell you the story of the battle of Lepanto..."

"Was it a sea-battle?" asked Gianni.

"Yes, it was one of the greatest battles I've ever seen in my long life. That battle was a great victory of the Republic of Venice."

"Who fought the battle?"

"The Venetians and their allies, mainly the Kingdom of Spain, against the fleet of the Ottoman Empire. "

"Ottoman? What's the meaning of this word?"

"Ottoman Empire was the name of the Turkish Empire," said Neptune. "The battle took place in 1571, in the sea in front of the Greek town of Lepanto. I saw the battle, I was there."

"Really?" asked Gianni, struck by that revelation. "In 1571?"

"Of course. Don't forget I'm a god from ancient Greece," replied Neptune with a mysterious smile. "The battle," he continued, "was fought between the ships of the Islamic Ottoman Empire," Neptune went on, "and the fleet of the Christian European countries. The galleys of Venice played a very important role in that battle."

"Galleys?" the boy asked. "What kind of ships were they?"

"They were battleships propelled by long lines of rowers", explained Neptune. "The galley is probably the oldest type of ship in history. The first large galleys appeared in ancient Egypt, and were used both as battleships and as cargo ships. Their name comes from the Greek word *galeos*, meaning *swordfish*. In fact, galleys were long and nimble, and they had a long iron pike in the front, just like a swordfish. That spike, in the course of battles, was a terrible weapon, able to sink an enemy ship. Galleys had a long line of cannons and many pieces of light artillery on each side. In addition, they had a cannon in the bow and one in the stern. There was a special reason why these ships were so slender."

"Maybe in order to penetrate more easily into the water?" asked Gianni.

"That's right," said the giant, "the energy produced by rowers was a limited resource, and a narrow hull makes the work of rowers easier. Speed is an important factor for a battleship, and the narrower the hull, the faster the ship can go. Venetians were very clever in building strong and innovative ships, so much so that other Mediterranean peoples, especially the Turks, copied them."

"Did the Turks also use galleys in the battle of Lepanto?"

"Yes, and their ships were well built, even though they were copied from the Venetian galleys they had captured. But Venice, in the battle of Lepanto, displayed a new, powerful war ship, the galleass."

"A much bigger galley, I suppose," said Gianni.

"Yes, of course, but not only bigger. It was the ultimate development of the Venetian galley. The galleass was a strange hybrid. Some years before the battle of Lepanto, the Ottoman Empire became increasingly threatening, and Venetians understood that war was near. In the *arsenale* - that was their shipyard - they had six large merchant galleys under construction. A navy strategist, looking at their powerful hull, got the idea of transforming that big commercial galley into a powerful warship. That was how the galleass was born."

"What does that name mean?" asked the boy.

"In the Venetian dialect *galea* is a galley, and *galeassa* is a bigger and stronger galea. Galleasses, being fitted out with a heavy artillery, had a great capacity of fire: they had a total of sixty cannons that could fire big balls of stone or iron. "

"Nevertheless, galleasses had a weak point, "continued Neptune, "they were slower than galleys. Venetians, therefore, made a great effort to increase the speed of their galleasses. They equipped them on each side with 32 oars, each worked by five rowers, instead of the 22-24 oars of the galley. And while galleys had one or two masts, galleasses had three of them. Anyhow, the galleass had a great advantage over the common galley, besides the power of artillery. They were higher, and from the upper deck the Venetian soldiers could dominate the enemies with a strong fire superiority."

"How many ships took part in the battle of Lepanto?" asked Gianni.

"Oh, a very large number, really," said Neptune. "I remember it very well. The Republic of Venice, the Spanish Kingdom, and their allies had a fleet of two hundred and six galleys and six galleasses," continued the giant. "One hundred and nine galleys, more than half of the total, and all the six galleasses, came from Venice. Forty-nine galleys came from Spain, twenty-seven from the Republic of Genoa. The other ships came from minor European states and military orders, such as the Knights of Malta."

"And what about the Ottoman Empire fleet?" asked Gianni.

"The Turks had a larger number of ships," said Neptune. "They had two hundred and thirty galleys and sixty galliots."

"Galliots?" said Gianni. "Were they another type of galley?"

"Yes, galliots were smaller galleys, in fact they were called *half-galleys*. This type of ship was used mainly by Algerian Barbary pirates, allied with the Turks. Galliots were faster and more maneuverable than galleys, and carried from two to ten cannons of small calibre. Of course, they were more vulnerable, so if they were caught under the fire of a Venetian galley's big cannons, they were doomed. The same things can be said about a battle fought between a galley and a galleass: faster the former, but far more powerful the latter."

"But tell me, Mr Neptune, why European countries decided to engage in a war between the Republic of Venice and the Ottoman Empire?"

"It's a long story," Neptune started to tell him. "For centuries the Republic of Venice and the Ottoman Empire had been at peace with each other. But at the beginning of the Fifteenth century things changed. The Turks wanted to expand the boundaries of their empire, and began to see in Venice's power, and its rich trades with the countries of the eastern Mediterranean area, a limit to their conquests. So they began to lay traps for the Venetian ships, making sudden attacks on its possessions, and hindering its commerce in every possible way.

In any case, Turks knew very well that the Republic of Venice wasn't, even for them, an easy target. They knew, for instance, that the commercial empire of Venice was founded on the power and efficiency of its fleet. The first move against Venice was made by the Ottoman Empire in March 1570, when the Sultan Selim II sent three hundred thousand men under the command of the general Mustapha Pasha to attack the island of Cyprus, a possession of Venice."

"After a month's fighting," went on Neptune, the Turks conquered Nicosia, the capital of Cyprus, and after five months' valiant resistance, the last fortress, Famagusta, fell.

But the Turks didn't limit themselves to attacking Cyprus. They sailed up the Adriatic Sea, plundering the coast, until they were a day's sailing time from Venice.

War, at this point, became inevitable. Faced with this alarming danger, the Venetians organized their defence. They barred the entry to the lagoon with a great chain, and behind the chain they moored numerous ships, all heavily armed. Hundreds of artillery-men and soldiers were put on guard at the Lido and in the fortresses of the lagoon."

"But was the Turkish army really so feared?" asked Gianni.

"Yes, at the beginning of the Sixteenth Century, the advance of Ottoman power frightened the whole of Europe, so much so that soon the King of Spain, The Republic of Genoa, the Knights of Malta, and other princes, decided to pool their ships and stand alongside Venice in its struggle against the Turks. In 1526 the armies of Suleiman conquered Hungary and in 1529 they beleaguered the town of Vienna, the capital of Austria. The Ottoman army was feared above all for the cruelty of its soldiers, the terrible Janissaries. The battle that the Venetians were going to fight was really a big one."

While Neptune was talking, Gianni had seen, gradually appearing on the surface of the water around the god's chariot, the weird heads of the Tritons and the delicate, turquoise-coloured faces of the Nereids. The creatures had clung to clumps of seaweed and stayed there rocking in the waves to listen to Neptune.

"The Turkish fleet was anchored in the Gulf of Lepanto, on the western coast of Greece," Neptune went on. "Its commander Ali Pasha was without worries. He waited calmly for the enemy fleet to arrive, feeling confident in the crushing superiority of his fleet. On 6th October 1571, Ali's look-out ships sighted the first enemy galleys. The fleet was at once

143

given the order to sail and line up in battle order. The commander of the Christian fleet, Don Juan, gave the same order."

"What was the battle order?" said Gianni.

"The Christian coalition fleet was divided into four divisions. The centre division had sixty-two galleys and was headed by Don Juan, who was on board the Spanish galley Real, together with Sebastiano Venier, later Doge of Venice. The left division had fifty galleys, mainly Venetian, and was led by Agostino Barbarigo. The right division consisted of 53 galleys under the command of the Genoese Giovanni Andrea Doria.

The six Venetian galleasses, with their heavy cannon batteries, were sent half a mile ahead of the Christian League's fleet, each of them in front of the three divisions. with the task of preventing the Turks from attacking the League's galleys with their fast galliots. The fourth division, lastly, was positioned behind the front line, as a reserve."

"But wasn't it dangerous to send the galleasses half a mile ahead against the whole Ottoman fleet?" asked Gianni.

"Not at all," replied Neptune: "On the contrary, it was a cunning trap. In fact, as soon as the battle began, the commander of the Turkish fleet Ali Pasha made a catastrophic error. Seeing those big, wide ships coming ahead of the League's fleet, he didn't realize that they were galleasses, the new Venetian battleships, but thought they were harmless supply ships, and decided to order an immediate attack. "

"I can imagine the consequences of this mistake..." said Gianni.

"Historians tell us that, that day, the galleasses sank up to seventy Turkish galleys and galliots. At the beginning of the battle the Venetian left division galleys were heavily attacked by the Turkish fleet, and were in big trouble, one of the reasons being that its commander Agostino Barbarigo had been killed by an arrow. The Venetians managed to react. They counterattacked and resisted until one of the galleasses came back from the front line and eliminated the assaulters. In addition, the centre division commanded by Don Juan had a hard clash with the Turkish centre division.

The terrible fight lasted five hours, and ended with a complete victory of the Christian fleet. Despite all the losses suffered, the Ottoman Empire managed to rebuild its fleet in the following years. Having seen the efficacy of the Venetian galleasses in the battle of Lepanto, the Turks decided to imitate them, and also built eight of these ships. In any case, they gave up trying to conquer Venice and Italian territories."

Neptune stopped. His deep dark eyes turned and looked at Gianni. "There you are, my boy" he said. "That was the battle of Lepanto, whose victory allowed Venice to save its culture, its traditions and its beauty."

Only then, seeing the sun that was setting, Gianni realized that it was late, too late.

"Sorry, Mr Neptune, I must go," he said to the giant. "My father will be waiting for me."

"Good luck, my boy," said Neptune, caressing Gianni's head with his big hand, "and keep in mind : no more underwater fishing."

"You have my word," Gianni said.

The sea horses drove the chariot to Lido Beach. Gianni ran to his beach hut, took his wet suit off, got dressed and ran to the hotel. The receptionist told him that his father had left a message for him. He had gone to Venice with his friends, and if Gianni wanted to join them, he could call him on the phone.

His father told him that he was in St Mark's Square, sitting down with his friends at a table outside the Florian Café.

"They have delicious ice-cream," said his father, "and there is also a small orchestra playing."

If Gianni took a vaporetto, added his father, he would reach St Mark's Square in less than half an hour.

Chapter sixteen

The long procession of followers and followed wandered through the narrow streets of Venice for a long time, that afternoon.

Alvin was undoubtedly the quickest of all of them: he only had to run for a few minutes for them to lose his tracks.

But the Peacocks didn't give up.

Half an hour went by, and the dog sighted them once again. A new flight, a new chase, and so it went on, a continual sequence of running, slowing down, and occasionally resting for a while.

It was enough to drive you mad.

"If you're prepared to forget about that little obnoxious beast," Edward said to his wife when it got too much for him, "I'll give you a Peruvian sable as a present."

"I forbid you to call Alvin *a little obnoxious beast*," she replied.

"I'll give you a handbag of iguana leather."

"No."

"Four white dachshunds."

"No."

"An Abyssinian cat."

It was no use insisting. Matilda wanted her little black and white dog. Nothing else would do.

The only one who was cheerful - besides Alvin of course - was Gea. Even though it was a bit tiring, she had really enjoyed the long race across the city.

As the sun sank lower and lower, Lady Matilda's despair increased. She was beginning to lose all hope of seeing Alvin again.

Gea, unwillingly, decided that it was time to put an end to the game and catch Alvin.

She left her parents, made a wide but quick detour through the lanes and then slowed down, walking on tiptoe. If she was right, Alvin should be more or less about here.

There he was, in fact, in a blind alley, absorbed in playing with an old rubber ball!

When he saw his young mistress blocking his escape, he gave a start of surprise. Then he stretched out his paws in front of him and began wagging his tail happily. But one look at his crafty gleaming eyes would have shown her that he was ready to run for it, given the chance.

"Alvin, aren't you tired of that game yet?" asked Gea.

"No, not at all," replied Alvin. "For the first time in my life, I'm having a lot of fun!"

"But aren't you happy that you live with us?"

"I'm a dog, not a rag doll!"

"Believe me, Alvin," said Gea. "We're doing all our best to make you happy."

"You're doing the best *for you*, not for me."

"So what do you want?"

"Let me tell you what I don't want," replied Alvin, always keeping a certain distance from Gea. "I don't like showers. I don't like being perfumed like a Hollywood poodle. I don't like candies, sweets and chocolates. I don't like tea and biscuits. I don't like carpets and sofas. I don't like cars. I would like to be a dirty, smelly Venetian dog, running all over the place with a load of bad, filthy cats to quarrel with."

"Be careful, Alvin! I've read that Venetians are very fond of their cats."

"Oh, I've found that out alright," said Alvin, smiling. "It's great being chased off by the Venetian fishmongers waving their terrible brooms at me - you should try it!"

"But you can't just go and do things like that!" protested Gea. "You're a well-behaved dog, from a good family."

"*You're* from a good family. I'm just a dog."

Gea was silent and thoughtful for a while. "Maybe you're right." She said. "Listen to me, Alvin. Why don't you try to explain that to mum or dad?"

"I've tried to, a thousand times! But you know as well as I do that only children, in certain cases, can understand us animals when we speak. In some other rare cases, young girls and boys can still hear what we're saying, but by the time you humans are adults, you can't hear us any more. You'll see - it will happen to you as well. When I try to tell your mum something, all I get back is: "*Alvin, for God's sake, stop barking like that!*"

"Ok, I'll try to explain that to mum for you," said Gea. "Now we really need to go back."

"No," replied Alvin. "Not yet."

The girl pointed to the ground. "Alvin, that's enough now! Come here!"

"Oooh hoo, what a nasty face you're making!" the dog teased her.

"It's a lot nicer than yours, Alvin. Have you seen yourself in a mirror lately? You look like a little wild pig!"

"What a lovely life I'm having with no baths…"

"Don't overdo it, Alvin. You're not getting away this time." Slowly the girl edged toward him…

The dog felt utterly trapped. "OK, let's make a deal," he said.

"What deal?"

"Let me get away now, and I'll let you catch me tomorrow."

"No way."

149

"Didn't you enjoy chasing me? It was great fun, wasn't it?"

"Well, yes, it was… but now mum is about to have a nervous breakdown."

"I wouldn't go very far in any case."

"Where would you go?"

"Over there, look…" Alvin's eyes seemed to grow sharper.

Gea turned to look.

In a flash the dog had brushed past her and was off, running away at full speed.

The girl took up the chase immediately, keeping right behind Alvin, until they reached a vast stretch of water.

A vaporetto was just leaving the landing-stage there. Alvin streaked along the landing-stage and sprang onto the. boat. He'd made it!

The vaporetto moved away quickly, and all Gea could do was to read its destination board: *Murano*. The island of Murano, home of the famous, ancient glassmakers.

Gea, disappointed, went back to her parents. Once she'd explained what had happened, they all returned to the landing stage, but on reading the timetable they realised that there would be no more launches going to Murano before the following morning.

They looked around, but they couldn't see anything that might take them to the island - there was not a gondola or a free motorboat, or indeed anything that floated, was in sight.

"So where do we go from here?" Matilda asked.

Edward shrugged. "It's not looking good to me. On the other hand, there's no way I'm swimming to the island."

They talked for a few minutes, trying to find a solution, but it quickly became clear that, at least for that evening, there was nothing they could do.

At last, while they were going away from the landing stage, Matilda took a last look at the sea, and suddenly stopped.

"Hey, Edward, Gea," she cried, "look over there!"

A lone gondola had appeared in the distance.

They came back and waited. The gondola was approaching, but very slowly. On board, there was a large-built man wearing a magnificent gondolier's costume. He had unmistakable carroty-red hair, a simple smile and a tattoo on his right arm.

A smothered cry came from the corner of a lane: "Muscleton! Yes… yes, it's him!"

Rubino and Volauvent rushed into the open and came right to the water's edge, without giving the Peacocks a second glance.

"As a matter of fact *we* saw that gondola first," said Lady Matilda, resolutely.

Volauvent, embarrassed, turned towards the woman. "What? Oh… oh yes, of course. But we can all get in, you'll see…"

Muscleton arrived in front of them and brought the boat alongside the landing stage. "Gondola, ladies and gentlemen?" he said, smiling as always.

Edward, of course, immediately recognized the three fellows he'd met in the tavern, but since Matilda wasn't happy about his new acquaintances in the field of Venetian taverns, he pretended he didn't know them.

Rubino and Volauvent, who had been prepared for anything except seeing Muscleton a free man again, were itching with curiosity. They made quick, sly gestures to the big man, who replied with grimaces that were meant to express something, but in fact told them nothing.

At last Rubino couldn't stand it anymore. He came close to Muscleton and whispered: "So, what happened to you, then?"

"Nothing happened to me," hissed back Muscleton. "Where did *you* get to? Or better still: why did you run away from the costume house?"

"There was somebody coming…"

"No, there wasn't. Nobody came. I chose this costume in peace and quiet, and thanks to being dressed like this I managed to get hold of a gondola and come looking for you. That's all."

Satisfied, Rubino got in the gondola, and so did Volauvent and the Peacocks, getting settled as best as they could.

The gondola left the landing-stage and slowly moved out onto the open water.

Throughout the crossing, the passengers had plenty of time to study their strange travel companions. Lady Matilda was particularly fascinated by the huge gondolier, while Gea watched the two strangely disguised thieves with curiosity, studying all their gestures and grimaces in great detail.

The sun set, and after a lazy twilight, darkness came.

Of course Muscleton didn't know where he was going. Until then, he had been aiming at random islands, but as the sun went down, he was completely at loss.

"Excuse me, mister gondolier, you're meant to be taking us to the island of Murano," said Lady Matilda. "But where on earth are you going?"

"Er…hum… "muttered Muscleton, " I'm sort of heading for those lights, over there."

"What are they?" demanded Lady Matilda. .

"Er… the lights of Murano, I… I think."

It was a chaotic night. Luckily, the moonlight helped them.

More than once they got stranded on sand-banks, and to get out again the men had to take turns in the water at pushing the boat.

It was nearly dawn when, thanks to a miracle that could only happen in Venice, they reached the island of Murano.

They were exhausted, pale as ghosts, their hair all over the place.

When they finally got off the boat, they understood how Christopher Columbus must have felt when he landed on the shores of America.

Chapter seventeen

It was the hour when the sun, having reached its highest point in the sky, seems to stop in its tracks and pour an immense cascade of heat and light onto the Earth.

St Mark's Square was almost deserted, apart from a few small groups of tourists who wandered slowly in the cool shade of the arcades.

Around the Lion, in the shade of his outspread wings, a group of birds were dozing, and among them there was Phoebus.

A flock of seagulls skimmed over the top of the column, and flew towards the Grand Canal.

The Lion followed them with his glance. "Ah... if only I could fly too, instead of being stuck up here all the time under the sun..." he sighed.

"You've got wings to fly with," said Phoebus, who was the only one still awake among the pigeons on the pedestal. "Why don't you give it a try?"

"Oh sure, and if it turned out I couldn't? It's not exactly easy, at my age, trying to fly for the first time."

"You mean to say you've never flown before?"

As an answer, the Lion raised his wings and beat them one against the other, making a deep clanging noise. "Can you hear that? They're made of bronze, not feathers."

The sound had woken the pigeons, who looked round curiously.

"If you really wanted to fly," Phoebus insisted, "you could do it, even with wings of lead."

"I'd *like* to try, but what would happen if I couldn't stay up in the air? And what if I couldn't come back on my column? Just imagine, me, the Lion of St Mark's, among dogs and cats, with the children jumping on my back and the tourists giving me peanuts! Oh the shame of it, I couldn't stand it!"

"But you never know, you could be really good at flying," said another pigeon. "Just think. One day you'd be on the domes of the Basilica, another day you could pop up to the Archangel Gabriel, and on another we could all go and visit Colleoni together..."

"Oh yes, I know, it'd be wonderful..." The Lion looked at the sky mournfully. "But how could I ever take the plunge? I mean, I might be able to if there was a good enough reason, something urgent..."

"And there's never been anything like that in all the years you've been here?"

The Lion pursed his lips, thinking about the question. "Well, yes, there has," he finally answered. "There was once a time when I very nearly took the great decision."

"Will you tell us about it?" Phoebus asked at once.

"It happened at Carnival time," the Lion begun, "a long, long time ago, when Venice was still at war with the Turks."

The pigeons came out from the shade of his wings and lined up in front of him, as they always did when a story was in the offing.

"Oh yes, mister Lion!" said a pigeon. "Tell us about how you nearly flew!"

"Well, the Venice Carnival, as you know," began to tell the Lion, "was a splendid event that lasted many days and attracted lots of visitors from all over Italy and Europe." The Lion turned to Phoebus. "Archangel Gabriel told you about it, didn't he?"

"Yes, he described Carnival Thursday: the *Flight of the Turk*, the fireworks, the acrobatics on top of the bell tower ..."

"Well then, the Sunday after that festival was the last day of Carnival," the Lion went on. "It was the last, but it was also the most joyous and the craziest. The streets were full of men, women and children in fancy dress.

The inns, the coffee-houses and the wine-shops were packed. But the most striking place in the whole city, where the people thronged in an incredible mass, was St Mark's Square. With all their grace and fantasy, how good the Venetians were at inventing and wearing fancy dress! The most famous costume, which in Venice was worn not only at Carnival but also for most of the year, was called *Tabarro e Bauta*.

It consisted of a long cloak, usually white or scarlet, over which was worn a black silk domino, that is, a hooded cape that covered the head and came down to the elbow, leaving only the face free. To complete the costume there was a two- or three-cornered hat and a velvet mask in black or white. The *Tabarro e Bauta* was very elegant, and the nobles used to wear it on other occasions, too, such as going to a reception or the theatre.

"A strange custom," said Phoebus. "Why did they do that?"

"The Republic of Venice, thanks to its trade with the eastern Mediterranean countries," explained the Lion, "was in those times the richest country in the world. Its citizens were businessmen, and probably they wanted to keep their names, their meetings and their financial interests secret. The same thing happens today, even if without masks.

The fantasy of the Venetians, however, really came into full play in the other costumes, those made famous by the Italian playwright Goldoni in his comedies: *Arlecchino*, with his checked suits of different coloured squares; *Pulcinella*, in his loose white smock and cone-shaped hat; *Brighella*, in a white dress with horizontal green stripes.

All these characters, and many others, wore masques, and were the typical protagonists of the *Commedia dell'Arte*, an ancient traditional Italian form of improvisational theatre."

"Impro... provi..." stammered Phoebus. "What's the meaning of this strange word?"

"Improvisational theatre," explained the Lion, "means that actors don't have to memorize a text, but must invent their dialogues on the spot. The Venetian Carnival, in fact, was a sort of great, general Comedy of Art. Try to imagine the scene. There were men dressed up as devils, doctors, Turks, coachmen, swaggering captains, poets or astrologers. The noisiest and wildest ones were of course the young men. Many of them disguised themselves as wet-nurses, maids, old women, and walked along chattering in shrill voices. Others, dressed up as babies, were taken for rides in a wheelbarrow, crying and kicking up noisy tantrums.

The "candy costumes" were funny, too. They were so called because if you wore one, you carried around a pole with a string tied to it and a big candy on the end of the string. Whoever managed to trap the candy with his mouth without using his hands, could eat it.

"Do they still hold a Carnival in Venice?" asked Phoebus, who was really interested in knowing, and seeing in real life, what the Lion was talking about.

"Yes, it's still going, but it's less spectacular in comparison with how it was years ago. Once, people were much merrier and light-hearted than they are now." The Lion shook his head slightly as if to say that he didn't approve of the turn things had taken. Then, he continued his account.

"So St Mark's Square, the last day of Carnival, was turned into a vast theatre where anybody and everybody could perform. Many stages were set up where singers, jugglers, actors and musicians did their acts. There were kiosks where, for a small fee, you could see puppet-shows, conjurers, wild beasts in cages, tight-rope walkers, astrologers and charlatans who sold miraculous remedies which could cure practically every kind of illness.

And if anyone would be doubtful and hesitating at the entrance to these travelling theatres, the showman was ready to sing the praises of what people would see inside. Leaning out of their improvised booths, there were wizards who could tell the secret fate held in store for you. There were tooth-drawers, makers of philtres and beauty creams, there were chemists who claimed they could obtain gold from mercury, and to prove it were busying themselves among crucibles, bellows and strange bottles. And all this went on in an indescribable confusion of voices, sounds, colours..."

"Mr Lion, just before, you said that during a Carnival you almost decided to fly," a pigeon reminded him. "Can you tell us what happened?"

"It was a very serious thing that nobody else noticed," the Lion explained. "Being up here, I was the only one who could see what was going on. It was Sunday and the sun had just set, leaving a strange violet light in the sky. There were still a few hours left to the end of Carnival, and the people, as if to make it last longer, were throwing themselves into the dances, games, jokes and pranks with a gaiety that became more and more frenzied."

"Suddenly, from the darkness of the lagoon, I saw a small sailing vessel emerging, a Turkish felucca," the Lion started to say once more. "Three men landed from it wearing turbans, puffy pants, babouches with curved points, and brilliant satin garments. One of them, the chief, carried two silver scimitars in his belt. With a slow, solemn gait they came into the glow of the torches lightning up the palaces, and approached the crowd.

When the people saw them, many stopped dancing just to have a look, and others gathered round. Some of the onlookers broke into applause. «Come and see what lovely costumes!» they called, and a chorus of approval ran through the crowd. «They look just like real Turks!», «Hey, those scimitars are sharp…», «And have you noticed their style of dancing? They look real!»

Someone asked the men where they'd found such splendid costumes, and got the reply: «*Mahmüt azim jawarkum ak mirmet.*» A roar of appreciation went up around them. «How clever they are! Did you hear them pretending to speak Turkish?» the by-standers asked each other, overjoyed at the joke. The three Turks tried to get away by mingling with the crowd, but by now the people had singled them out, and nobody wanted to miss the amusement they promised. «Show us a traditional dance of your country!» somebody shouted.

Laughing, the crowd made a space around them - in vain, however, because the three were still impassive. «Aha, they're making out they don't understand us!» yelled a man, and, to play along with the joke, did a few dance steps in front of them. «*Ak uhrut!*» the Turks exclaimed. Finally, with great agility, they improvised a Moorish dance, beating their heels together and the chief whirling his scimitar over his head."

The Lion rested for a while, then started to tell the story again. "Gradually, as I watched the scene unfolding below me, a strange idea ran through my head: and if the three of them were *really* Turks? What if they'd come to Venice as spies, taking advantage of the Carnival to act unobserved?

Then, just as I was trying to answer these questions, the three Turks finished their dance, and weaving their way

159

through the crowd, managed to break away and get a moment for themselves. They came right to the foot of my column and began muttering rapidly to one another. Well, as you know I come from the East, and I could still remember a few words of Turkish, so I tried to understand something of their conversation.

One was called Omar, and the others Ali and Rashid. They were talking about maps, pashas in prison, poisons, rope ladders and other devilish contrivances, and seemed rather annoyed at the heathens for not leaving them in peace. When I heard their words, my suspicions were confirmed. The three weird characters were real Turks, and spies into the bargain!

I crouched on my pedestal and poked my neck down to get a better view of what they were going to do. The trio moved towards the square again, with the intention of slipping into the crowd without being noticed, among the thousands of people in costumes. Their attempt was useless: their clothes were too splendid, too real not to arouse general admiration and curiosity.

Once again they were welcomed, made to dance, forced to take part in the candy-catching game. A Pulcinella arrived with a flask of wine, and offered it to the Turks. At first they refused it, but then, gasping after their dances, drank with a will. After this, arm in arm with a troupe of devils, old women and harlequins, they began parading round the square, yelling out mysterious oriental singsongs.

It was difficult not losing sight of them in that chaos, but with a lot of patience I managed. At last I realized that the three of them weren't able to get away from their roistering companions for the rest of Carnival. Midnight came. The great bell of St Mark's with its deep bronze voice announced that Carnival was over. Little by little the large square began to empty of people. The charlatans put out the fires under their crucibles, the wizards took down their booths, the conjurers put away their rabbits and magic hats, the puppeteers laid their tiny wooden actors carefully in their boxes. Only a few groups of tenacious merrymakers were left behind, trying until the last minute to keep the party going.

Omar, Ali and Rashid were left behind too, forced to remain together with the last upholders of the Carnival. Yet, inevitably, after a few hours, the groups thinned out and broke up. The last torches were put out and the square was left silent under the pale beams of the moon. The Turks, however, had not gone away. Their felucca was proof enough of this - it was rocking in the waves beside the quay, its sails furled on the spars.

I started looking around, scrutinizing the long shadows in which the square was steeped. There was no one in sight. Time passed and I twisted and turned restlessly on the pedestal, trying to imagine what the devil the Turks were doing at the moment. The moon set, and towards the east the sky began to brighten.

It was then that all of a sudden I caught sight of the unmistakeable profiles of the three men, creeping on tiptoe along the roof of the Doge's Palace. Omar took out a scroll-map, unrolled it and referring to it from time to time, the three of them began to walk up and down, measuring the distance with their strides. From their gestures, I understood what they were up to: they were looking for the right spot to take some tiles off and lower themselves into the palace!

The brightness to the east was spreading and becoming stronger. The Turks stopped for a moment, looking anxiously at the light, then, more frantically than ever, they started measuring again. In the end they must have found the place they wanted because, putting the map down on the roof, they bent down and began removing the first tiles.

At that moment, my friends, I knew I had to do something: I had to detach myself from this pedestal and try to fly, reach the spies and frighten them away. I was just about to move when Omar, struggling to lift a tile, accidentally kicked the map. The parchment scroll rolled down the roof, slipped through the white battlements on top of the façade and dropped into space. The three Turks, who had tried to chase it, beat their fists on their turbans in despair. But their despair was even greater when they noticed that the sky was now flooded with pink light, the stars had gone out, and the shadows were before the sun. Their exploit had failed.

They lowered a rope ladder from the roof and scrambled down as fast as their legs would carry them. Once down they ran to search for the map, but, alas, it was not there. In falling, it had been blown away by the wind, got lodged in the hand of a statue, and there it stayed, high up on the façade of the nearby St Mark's Basilica, pointing towards the sky. With a final gesture of irritation, Omar and his two servants turned and strode for their ship. When they had freed the mooring rope, they unfurled the sails and in a short time, driven by the morning breeze, the felucca was out of sight. There you are, my friends. That was the only time I almost decided to fly."

The Lion had finished his story.

In silence Phoebus and his friends moved back into the shade of his wings.

In front of them, side by side along the quay, the shining gondolas were rocking on the water, the bows stretching upwards like swans' necks. The waves were gently slapping against their wooden sides with a hollow noise.

Lulled by this familiar, quiet sound, the pigeons crouched down on the pedestal and dropped off to sleep.

162

Chapter eighte

As soon as they landed on the islai.
Peacocks had taken a rest after all the hards.
crossing. They had had breakfast and then, fol.
distance by the thieves, had started wandering rc
narrow lanes of the island.

Even if they were worried about the flight of A.
and her parents couldn't help being enchanted by the
picturesque streets and houses of Murano.

All of them, now, were on an island. Alvin certainly
couldn't escape them this time.

The Peacocks went down for quite a while searching
every nook and cranny, every possible hiding-place. The dog,
as usual, had disappeared.

They saw a group of tourists going into an old building,
and without quite knowing why, they tailed after them,
having now decided to explore the island from top to bottom.

The intense heat, the reflection of the flames on the high
ceilings, and the conversation of the people around them at
once made it clear that they were inside a glass factory.

Next to the open furnaces, which gave off a blinding
light, the craftsmen were working with steady, sure
movements. By means of long metal rods they were placing
blocks of glass of every shape and colour into the furnace,
where they turned them over and over until the glass became
white-hot, then they extracted it and held it out to the master
glassmakers, who were sitting nearby.

With pincers of different sizes, shears, and large
syringes full of water, these masters bustled round the piece of
incandescent glass, stretching or shortening it as they wished,
cutting away the superfluous parts and rounding off the

The glass, soft and pliable like marzipan, took on
ery odd shapes.

Other workmen blew through the metal rods until the
of glass sticking to the rod's end began to swell slowly.
w one of the master-craftsmen took over and with some
nning snipping and snapping with the pincers corrected the
hape, soon turning it into the required object - a vase, a bird,
a chalice, a bottle…

"The art of glass-making has very ancient origins in
Venice," a guide was saying meanwhile to a group of tourists.
"Over a thousand years ago, they had begun making *tesserae*,
as the small square pieces of coloured glass like those used for
the mosaics in St Mark's are called. At the end of the
Fourteenth century, because of the danger of fires and in order
to get rid of the smoke, the glassmakers' furnaces were moved
from Venice to the Isle of Murano, where they still stand. And
since, in practice, the fires are never put out, you can say that
these furnaces have been alight for seven hundred years."

The visitors passed on to a nearby hall where the most
beautiful objects produced at the factory were on display.
Many of these objects were antique and very delicately made.

"The move to the island of Murano," the guide went
on, "marked the beginning of a new and splendid period for
the Venetian glass-makers. In fact their activity became a
fully-fledged art, in no way inferior to painting and sculpture.
And bit by bit, as their experience was passed on from father
to son, but kept secret from the outside world, their work
became more and more skilled and refined. The master
glassmakers of Murano were so famous and so respected that
the Venetian government granted them special rights. One of
these was that their daughters could marry into the Venetian
nobility."

While the Peacocks walked round inside the glass-factory among the marvels of this ancient art, Rubino, Volauvent and Muscleton waited for them outside. The three thieves were worried, because they were pretty sure the new day would bring them a whole heap of trouble. Suddenly Rubino gave a start. He had seen the cause of all their troubles passing by a short distance away. It was the Peacocks' dog!

Angrily they dashed in pursuit of Alvin. The dog, for his part, recognized the two men straight away, and thinking back with terror to the leap they'd forced him to make from the Rialto bridge, he dashed off at breakneck speed.

At the first crossroads he turned left, ran a short way down the road, then, thinking he couldn't be seen, dived into a house. It was one of the many glasshouses on Murano.

The thieves went after him.

"Hey, where do you think you're going?" one of the glassblowers shouted in alarm, moving towards them. "What do you want?"

The dog had slipped into a large room and had taken shelter under one of the many cabinets, which were full of glassware. Immediately the three thieves rushed into the room and began poking round the cabinets, trying to unearth the fugitive.

At the far end of a large room, Alvin glimpsed a door ajar. This might be his salvation. Without a second's hesitation, he sprang out and ran towards it.

The crucial moment had come.

Muscleton pushed aside his companions, made a swift run-up and took off.

It was an incredible jump - epic, as only Muscleton's exploits could be. He flew several yards in the traditional pose of the flying angel, but since, unlike an angel, he was without wings, he was eventually forced to land.

With a desperate twist, Alvin avoided his clutches. Plowing through everything before him like an avalanche, the big man hit the side of a cabinet and sent it crashing down. The cabinet fell onto the one next to it, which knocked over the next one, and so on, like a tumbling pack of cards, accompanied by a deafening crash of glass shattering into a thousand pieces.

Not until all was silent and it was clear that not even the smallest liqueur glass had been saved from destruction did the three thieves, who had just stood there gazing open-mouthed, come to themselves again.

A second later the master glassmaker also came to himself, just in time to see the authors of the catastrophe dashing through the small door at the end of the room.

"Criminals! My glass!" he cried desperately. "A billion in damages at least!"

Alvin and the three thieves were running headlong through the crowded lanes of Murano.

They came within sight of a quay. The dog turned right, the thieves, rather, kept straight on. Dumbfounded, Alvin stopped and turned to watch them. Why on earth should they stop chasing him?

It was then that the dog noticed an astonishing fact as he watched the three men. They'd not only given up chasing him, but now *they* were running away!

In a split second the three of them had reached the quay. A quick look at the boats moored there, and they all jumped into a motor boat, started the motor and shot off at full speed for Venice. Rubino, Volauvent and Muscleton, as you might easily imagine, had decided to throw in the towel.

Now, sitting on the comfortable seat of the motor boat, they were at last able to relax.

"After all there's no shame in admitting you're beaten," said Rubino, who was steering the boat.

The other two found it quite easy to agree with him.

Volauvent dried the sweat from his forehead. "The important thing is to recognize defeat when you see it," he said. "It happened to Julius Caesar, Charlemagne and Napoleon. It could easily have happened to us, couldn't it?"

"It could," Rubino and Muscleton chorused.

The decision not to worry about the Peacocks and their dog gave them joy in living, and hope for the future again.

The nightmare was over.

They moored the boat at St Mark's quay, landed and walked through the square to a clothes shop. Soon after, they came out dressed as real tourists with gaudy shirts, white shorts and casual sandals. They went to a restaurant, where they relaxed enjoying good Venetian dishes, and then they had a pleasant, lazy stroll through the narrow streets of the centre. They bought three large ice-cream cones, and without a care in the world arrived in fabulous St Mark's Square.

At this point we'd better leave the three thieves to their Venetian pleasures and return to the Peacocks on Murano.

The island was small, and inevitably, walking here and there, the family came across their runaway dog.

The chase was short and fierce. Alvin made for the quay and jumped onto a vaporetto, but this time it didn't work.

The vaporetto, in fact, *was* going to leave, but at the moment it was still moored to the quay, so Edward, Matilda and Gea were able to come on board. After a while the mooring ropes were untied, the vaporetto left the wharf, and Alvin was trapped.

He took refuge on the roof of the wheelhouse, but when he saw some sailors climbing up to get him, that was out of question; he came down of his own free will and delivered himself to his masters' leash. Honourable surrender was better than shameful capture.

Matilda held Alvin up and looked into his eyes. "You cunning little devil, you! You stupid rascal!" said the woman, but not shouting, in fact with a quiet, low tone of voice, that was neither angry nor hateful.

Gea came close to her mother. "He isn't a nasty dog, mum," she said. "Don't be too unkind. He's here now, isn't he?"

"He's only here because we managed to catch him, the scamp, otherwise Lord knows where he would be now."

"I only wanted a little fun, " said Alvin

"He's with us again just because we managed to catch this scamp, otherwise Lord knows where he would be now."

"I only wanted a little fun, " repeated Alvin.

"No, you can stop your barking now," said Matilda. " Just shush and lie low. For a long time."

Alvin turned his muzzle to face Gea. "You see?" he said. "They don't understand me".

"Mum, Alvin didn't bark," said Gea. "He said something to you."

"Said something?" Matilda looked at her attentively. "Gea, darling, are you feeling alright?"

"Yes I am, mum," replied the girl. "Alvin tried to speak to you, but you didn't understand what he said. It always happens that way."

Matilda, still holding Alvin in the air, stared at Gea with a doubtful expression on her face. "So, what do you think he bar... what did he try to tell me just now?"

"He told you that he just wanted a little fun."

168

"Are you sure?"

"Believe me, mum. I know Alvin very well."

Matilda looked at her dog again, her eyes wet and full of love. "Oh my adorable beastly little puppy, my beloved runaway teddy bear!" she said, sobbing. "Sooner or later you'll break my poor heart!"

Clutching Alvin to her breast, she buried her nose in his coat. "My lovely hairy tramp, my..."

The woman got a whiff of her adorable pet. "Ooooah!" she yelped, holding the dog away from her face. "You smell like a monkey! You need to be washed in a bath full of cologne at once!"

Alvin barked.

"What did he say?" Matilda asked to Gea.

"Well... he said that next time..." replied Gea, giggling, "he'll escape to Africa aboard a cargo ship and take refuge with a tribe of baboons."

Edward decided to join in the discussion, "Matilda, darling, why don't we enjoy our holiday and let Gea take care of this beastly beast?"

"Good idea, dad," replied at once Gea. "I'll take him straight away to the nearest self-service dog wash. I saw one of them in Venice."

Alvin barked again.

"All right, Alvin," said Gea. "Just soap and water. No perfumes at all."

Now, at last, the Peacocks would also be able to enjoy their Venetian holiday in peace.

It was then that Edward looked around and began to mutter abruptly: "But... but... for goodness' sake, where are we going?"

Matilda looked around as well, and Gea did the same.

"Venice is there," said Gea, "but we are going in the opposite direction!"

"In fact, *where* are we going?" repeated Edward. "Well, I'll put the question to someone on the staff," he said.

When Edward came back after a few minutes, he was smiling. "No tragedy," he announced. "I've been informed that we are going to the island of Burano. According to them, it's a small, delightful Venetian island. We'll be there in forty five minutes."

"Thank goodness," said Matilda.

"I'll have a look at my travel book," said Gea. She sat down, opened her small backpack and pulled an e-book reader out of it. She made a quick search and after a while started reading. "First of all, an interesting fact: international travel magazines include Burano among the ten most colourful places in the world. Besides, Burano is famous for its marvellous handcrafted laces. It's worthwhile visiting the Lace Museum and the most colourful house of Burano, called La Ca' di Bepi, which means Joe's House."

The Peacocks found the visit to the village a charming experience. All those houses, painted in a wide range of bright colours, gave visitors the impression that they were in a kind of fairy toy-village whose inhabitants could be dressed with bold colours, too.

They took the vaporetto headed for Venice in the early afternoon, and since they arrived fairly early, they decided to stay on board, and go up and down the Grand Canal, looking at its beautiful palaces.

Gea, keeping Alvin's leash clenched around her wrist, opened her small electronic travel-book and read the names of some of the most beautiful palaces overlooking the canal.

"One of the most famous is *Ca' Dario*," Gea started reading. "Ca' Dario, which means Dario's House, took its name from the rich merchant Giovanni Dario, who built it in 1487.

This palace is famous for various reasons: for the beauty of its architecture and decorations, because it's tilted to the right, and, most of all, because of a legend which says that its owners, since the end of the 18th century, would be hit by misfortune."

"Matilda, please, don't ask me to buy this palace," joked Edward.

"For heaven's sake," replied Matilda. "I have no such intention!"

Gea read the descriptions of many other palaces, the *Ca' Rezzonico*, seat of a fine museum of the 18th century arts in Venice, the *Ca' d'Oro*, so-called for the gilded decorations on its façade, the *Ca' Foscari*, which hosted the University, *Ca' Giustinian*...

"Oh, I'm sorry, but now I'd better stop reading my book," said Gea suddenly, "otherwise, instead of looking at the palaces, I look at their photos!"

At the end of their beautiful tour along the Grand Canal, the Peacocks landed on the quay of St Mark' Square.

In was then that Matilda remembered an urgent need. Alvin required a good bath. It was late afternoon, though, and probably no pet shops were still open at that time. Matilda said that they could wait until tomorrow morning, but Edward didn't agree at all.

"I'd sleep in the bathroom rather than sleeping in the same bedroom with this stinking baboon," he said.

"Edward, you are forbidden to talk about Alvin like this!" replied Matilda.

"*You* said the same thing about Alvin," answered Edward.

"Yes," insisted Matilda, " but I..."

"Mum, excuse my interrupting you," Gea said. "I've seen a pet shop not far from here, I'll run down and see if they are still open!"

"Thank you, Gea, you are my angel!" said Edward.

"Come on, Alvin, hurry up!" Gea said to Alvin.

The pet shop was still open, but the shopkeeper told her that she was about to close.

"Oh, no, Madam, I implore you," said Gea. "My father threatened to sleep in the bathroom!"

"Your father what?" asked the shopkeeper, her eyes wide open.

"My father says that rather than sleeping in the same room with this dog he will sleep in the bathroom."

"But why doesn't he want to sleep with this dog? He seems so well-behaved, he looks like." The shopkeeper, suddenly, began to smell the air. "Hmm... I'm beginning to understand your father..."

"My father says that he stinks like a baboon..."

The shopkeeper bent a little - just a little - towards Alvin. "More than a baboon, I would say a pig... What's his name?"

"Alvin," replied Gea.

"Let's go, Alvin," the woman said.

Incredibly, Alvin let the shopkeeper bath him without complaining too much.

Gea reached her parents, then all of them went back to their hotel in the centre of Venice. At last they relaxed with a good shower and changed their clothes.

Later, the Peacock family had dinner at a restaurant on the Grand Canal. Lady Matilda ordered a plate of snails *à la Bourguignonne* for Alvin, who found them simply disgusting. Yet, wanting to obey to his masters, he displayed his impeccable manners by eating everything and licking the plate clean, as well.

At around ten o'clock, they went for a pleasant after-dinner walk in St Mark's Square, where they sat at a table outside the oldest café-bar in the world, the famous, historical Florian Café, opened in 1720. A small orchestra was playing.

In the meantime, Muscleton, Volauvent and Rubino, reached a corner of St Mark's Basilica and sat down on a marble bench, licking their ice-cream cones. Behind them, standing against a corner of the basilica, stood the black figures of the Four Moors, the legendary Saracen thieves who'd come to Venice in the old times to steal the Treasure of St Mark's.

When he'd finished his ice-cream, Rubino smiled at an idea that passed through his mind. "What a funny old world it is," he said. An international band of crooks, sensationally successful, defeated by one little dog…"

"International band? Sensationally successful?" asked Muscleton, ironically. "I didn't know we were an international band, or we had sensational successes."

"I'm thinking about our next job," said Volauvent. "In Barbara Button's villa in Miami, there's an art collection that's worth a fortune "

"You must be mad!" said Muscleton, shaking his big, red head. " We've just given up running after a flea-ridden little dog, and you start planning a job in…"

Rubino hushed him. "Ssssh! I heard something, a kind of… a kind of whisper…"

Suddenly, they heard a mysterious sigh, a breath that seemed to arise from secret depths.

"Hey… hey there…" murmured a voice.

The three of them spun around, astonished. Only the four statues, black and still, were there.

"Turn around as you were before," whispered one of the Moors, "and pretend you haven't heard anything."

Dumb with amazement, the thieves looked at each other.

"Turn around, I said!" the same statue commanded. This time the voice was sharp and biting. "Do you want people to notice?"

The three men, who had turned pale, goggled at the enigmatic stone figures, then obeyed the command.

"You're thieves, aren't you?"

"Er... well..." stuttered Rubino.

"You are, I heard you say you were. And there's no need to lie to us. But tell me, what kind of thieves are you? Just pickpockets or something on a higher level?"

Volauvent raised his right eyebrow, annoyed by the insinuation. "For your information, all the biggest jobs over the last five years have been our work."

Muscleton opened his eyes wide and puffed his cheeks out, as if he would stifle a laugh. Volauvent, at once, nudged him in the ribs.

"Good. Very good," said the mysterious voice. "We've been waiting for people like you for centuries."

The statue gave them a brief account of the Moor's history - how they'd come to Venice from distant lands, how they'd got into the treasure room, the marvellous things they'd found there, and finally their fatal quarrel over sharing all those riches...

"Now we want someone to get what we, for a trifle, let slip through our hands," the statue ended up. "Are you ready to steal the Treasure of St Mark's?"

Once again, the three looked at each other.

"Ste... stealing the Treasure of St Mark's?" stammered Muscleton. "And how cou... could we?"

"We know a secret passage that gives you direct entry to the treasure chamber. Listen…"

The thieves stood up and leaned backwards toward the statues, listening intently, anxious not to miss the smallest detail of what they were going to hear. And it was really worth it. In fact, they heard that by pushing a particular slab in the outer wall from left to right, and pressing the lower edge of another, they would open a passage that would take them straight into the treasure chamber. They had just to remember one small but rather thrilling problem: they had to be very careful, because there was great danger in that matter. Those who attempted to steal that treasure had a terrible curse weighing on their heads: the risk to be turned into a black stone statue.

"That's what happened to us, as you can see," said the talking statue. "We came to Venice from faraway lands in order to steal the treasure, but the guardians caught us and… here we are, turned into stone forever!"

Rubino, Muscleton and Volauvent once again looked at each other, frightened out of their wits. They talked the matter over among themselves, asking the Four Moors their opinion when necessary. In the end they decided they would carry out the great coup that very night, after midnight.

Chapter nineteen

The evening was a very pleasant one for the Peacocks. As for Alvin, at last he was behaving like a well-mannered dog. To show he had learned his lesson, he never yanked the leash held by Gea, and when they sat down at the table outside the café and she ordered him to lie down under her chair, the dog obeyed very quietly. Then, just in case, the girl picked up the leash and tied it around her chair leg.

Alvin soon began to show a rather worrying interest in the pigeons that crowded the square and wandered near the tables in search of crumbs. The temptation was very strong, and Alvin tried to resist with all his strength, but when one of the pigeons came near, too near, gazed at him straight in his eye, and made a strong "Coo-coo", Alvin lost his temper. Enough is enough, even for a dog who promised to behave himself. He jumped up and tried to catch the pigeon, but the leash blocked him in time.

After a while, another pigeon came close to Alvin, pecking at crumbs.

"Why do you all have to tease me," Alvin said to the pigeon, "When I decided to be a polite dog?"

Ignoring him completely, the pigeon continued its search. What Alvin couldn't know, is that the Florian Cafe's delicious cakes are well known in Venetian pigeon circles for producing a better class of crumb, so, of all the tables under which to go crumb hunting, Florian's is the undisputed favourite.

This was the reason why, at a certain point, the bird, engaged in crumb picking, didn't realize he was coming too close to the dog. Alvin, of course, jumped up again to catch the pigeon. It was useless, since the leash was too short.

Then another pigeon moved away from the group and stood in front of Alvin, just inches beyond the range of his leash.

"Hey you," said the bird, "why are you so mad at us?"

"I'm not mad at you," replied Alvin. "I just hate being disturbed by those non-stop coo-cooing noises while I'm sleeping."

"For a dog, you don't seem to be too clever."

Alvin's eyes narrowed to slits. "What exactly do you mean?"

"I mean that you are a little stupid," said the pigeon calmly.

Alvin drew back his lips, showing his teeth. "What's your name?" he snarled.

"I'm Phoebus, I'm a carrier pigeon."

"Listen to me, Phoebus-the-carrier-pigeon," growled Alvin. "You're asking for trouble."

"Oh, no, not at all, I don't like trouble," replied Phoebus. "I decided to remain in Venice just because it's a peaceful city: no cars, no eagles, no falcons, no hunters. Tell me your name."

"Alvin."

"Believe me, Alvin, I didn't mean to provoke you. It's just that I can't stand seeing animals treated like that."

Alvin was surprised. "How do you think I'm treated?"

"Badly," said Phoebus. "I don't understand how you dogs can accept a collar strapped around your neck, a leash attached to your collar, and a master who uses them to strangle you."

Alvin seemed to calm down. "Hmm... I agree with you. In fact, I hate both collar and leash. But..."

"But what?" asked Phoebus.

177

"But I must say that it's usually me who pulls on the leash, or stops refusing to go ahead, or who wants to cross the road even if my masters don't. I'm not an easy chap, you know."

"Anyway, you don't have to jump about like a wild thing if you want to free yourself," said the pigeon. "The more you jump, the more the knot tightens. You'll end up strangling yourself."

"So what do you suggest?" asked Alvin.

"I'll give you a tip only if you promise me that you won't dash about among us all..."

"I promise."

"All right, Alvin. Think about it. Your masters tied your leash around a chair leg, so all you have to do is untie yourself. You have good teeth and I bet it will be an easy little job, for you."

"Hmm... good idea."

"Now I've to go," said Phoebus. "Friends forever?"

"Sure, friends forever," replied Alvin, lying down again under the chair.

Lulled by the sweet, romantic music of the Florian Cafe's small orchestra, Alvin fell asleep.

A garland of lights crowned the palaces around the great square, making the marble shine, and outlining the profiles of the columns, arches and statues.

From time to time a light breeze scented with the nearby sea rustled through the square, raising the music from the café orchestras and carrying it far away over the city.

Fate is always mixing things in life without order or logic. But at times, mysteriously, it amuses itself by drawing together the invisible threads that keep men attached to it, just

178

as a puppet-master might suddenly lift all his puppets in the air and make a single bunch of them.

This is what happened that night in St Mark's Square.

Around eleven o' clock, chattering and laughing, a large group of eccentric celebrities arrived at the Florian Café. Among many others, there were Gianni and his father, Bob Webster, the great producer, with the famous actress Stella Dawn and a group of starlets. Then, followed by her butler in red livery came Gloria Simpson, the celebrated star of the past, engaged in an endless conversation with Grand Duchess Greta of Hapsburg. The photographer David Healey and his towering models were there, as well as the Emir of Kubai, the banker von Klumpfen, the Texan oilman Joe Bass, and a wild horde of fans, autograph hounds, onlookers and paparazzi.

All these people, except the paparazzi, onlookers and autograph hounds, sat down at the tables of the Florian Café. Gianni, sitting at the same table with his father, Bob Webster, and Stella Dawn, saw that he happened to be near a table where a young girl was eating a big ice-cream.

Gianni turned towards her. "Is it good?" he asked.

"Eh... what?" replied the girl, somewhat surprised.

"The ice-cream."

"Oh, I thought you meant my dog," said Gea, smiling, and pointing to Alvin, who was sleeping under her chair. "No, my dog isn't so good. The ice-cream, however, is delightful."

"Then I'll have the same, too," said Gianni. "The ice-cream, I mean, not the dog. Though, I must say, I like your dog very much. He's a fox-terrier, isn't he?"

" Yes, he is. Not an easy dog, actually."

"Really? He would seem so handsome and so funny with his moustache and beard..."

"That's just his face," said Gea. "He's a little devil really."

Alvin, still asleep, raised an ear.

"What a pity!" said Gianni. "I would like to have a dog like him!"

"Oh, I don't mean that fox-terriers are bad or stupid. He's playful, especially with balls, he's curious, clever, and he adores running. He's also a great watchdog."

"But...?" asked Gianni.

Alvin raised the other ear.

"But he's terribly stubborn."

"And?"

"Quarrelsome."

Alvin opened one eye,

"What else?"

"He's always ready to pick a quarrel with other animals, even if they are much larger than him. So, sometimes he gets a good beating. But...bad or good, he's my dog, and I love him."

Alvin closed his eye, lowered his ears and went on sleeping.

"What's your name?" Gianni asked.

"Gea," she replied. "I come from England. And you?"

"Gianni."

"It's an Italian name, isn't it?"

"Yes, it is. In English my name sounds like Johnny."

"I'm sorry to interrupt your conversation," said Lady Matilda, "but Gea, darling, if you don't eat your ice-cream, it will melt."

"Oh, I'm sorry, it's my fault," said Gianni.

"No, it's mine," said Gea, getting on with her ice-cream.

It was just a few minutes before midnight, and although a lot of people were still milling around the center of

Venice, the crowd had begun to thin out. It was a perfect, clear summer night. A smooth, fresh breeze coming from the sea flowed into the great square and mixed with the music from the open-air cafés, carrying it skyward.

The heavy tones of the big bell announced that it was midnight.

"Hmm, there are still too many people around," said Volauvent. "I think it would be better to wait a little longer."

"But... are you sure?" asked Muscleton.

"Sure of what?" asked Volauvent.

"Sure about this job," replied the big man. "I don't want to become a black stone statue."

"What about a white marble statue?" joked Volauvent.

"Well, it could be a fine monument," said Muscleton. "But I fear that if they caught us, they wouldn't dedicate marble monuments to us. They would rather transform us into stone statues"."

"Are you really so superstitious?" asked Volauvent.

"I don't know," said Rubino, "But if these things were just superstitions, statues wouldn't speak."

"Don't be too surprised at what you see and hear in Venice," replied Volauvent." There are a lot of weird things here: lions with wings, four horses high up on the basilica façade, high tide in the streets, over four hundred bridges, boatmen who row standing instead of sitting, no buses, no subways only waterbuses... Is it even a real city?"

The three thieves discussed for a good half an hour whether or not they were prepared to risk being arrested and turned into statues. They agreed on one thing only: it didn't matter if the stone was black or white. At last they found that the only solution was to make their minds up there and then, once they'd taken a look at the treasure.

Shortly afterwards, three black figures crept through the shadows along the side of St Mark's Basilica. They halted near a corner of the building. The biggest of the three was carrying a couple of big empty sacks under his arm.

They busied themselves around two marble slabs fixed in the side of the Basilica. It took them a while to find the right point in each slab, but they finally succeeded.

A third slab slowly opened upon itself like a window, revealing a dark, narrow passage. Rubino, Volauvent and Muscleton entered quickly, closing the heavy slab behind them. By the light of an electric torch they crawled forward on all fours until they found their way barred by a wall of marble.

They pushed, and it gently swung open.

The torchlight explored a large table full of antique pieces of gold, silver, enamel, and jewels - a fabulous collection of valuable items: statuettes, chalices, candlesticks, vases, crosses, goblets, caskets…

Volauvent, handling the torchlight, lit up the precious objects one by one. He and his friends. standing at the entrance, were frozen to the spot, their mouths half-open in a long gasp of amazement.

"Do you think there is an alarm system?" asked Muscleton.

Volauvent explored the stone walls and the ceiling with the torchlight. "No sensors," he said. "No video recorders, just a lot of cobwebs."

"And there are no entrance doors either..." added Rubino.

"Hey, look at those pieces on the table," said Muscleton. "They are so dusty!"

"You're, right..." said Volauvent. "St Mark's Treasure is a museum open to visitors. This can't be a part of the museum, with all that dust! It looks as if it's a secret room that's been closed for centuries."

"So we can take it all," said Rubino. "and no one will notice."

"All right, let's just stay calm shall we," said Volauvent. "Do you think we could cross the whole city unseen with two big sacks full of rattling gold pieces on our shoulders?".

"Well, we can't give up now!" protested Muscleton.

"I tell you, it's not a good idea," replied Volauvent. "Remember the statues..."

"So?" asked Rubino.

"Well, I was just thinking..."

Nobody in St Mark's Square had noticed the three thieves, their long search round the Basilica's marble slabs, or their entering the passage.

Nobody, except for the statue of Justice.

While all the other statues and the birds had long since been lulled to sleep by the soft music from the orchestras, Justice had stayed awake, vigilant as always.

From high up on the Doge's Palace, she kept watch over the square, severe and attentive as she always was.

When she saw the three thieves at work, she was so shocked that she nearly lost her grip on her huge sword. As soon as she'd recovered, she looked round in search of help, and immediately her glance fell on the trays of the scales she was holding in one hand.

With their heads under their wings, each in his own tray, two pigeons were sleeping.

"Hey, wake up!" hissed Justice, raising the scales up to her face and shaking them a little.

The pigeons drew their heads from under their wings and opened their eyes wide in the half-light.

"What's happening?" one of them asked.

Justice explained to them and added hurriedly: "You must fly to the other birds at once, wake them up, and tell them to wake all the other statues… Quick, off you go!"

With a swift hop, the two pigeons dived into the night.

The birds they woke up warned others in turn, and the process continued and spread until there was a swarming jostling mass of pigeons, an overlapping of cooing and twittering, and a restless fluttering of wings on all the buildings in the square.

"They're stealing St Mark's Treasure!" The whisper echoed among the spires, over the domes and around the statues.

"The Treasure? How?"

"We don't know. Quick, quick!"

"There's a secret passage…"

"They've got in through a window!"

"But how many of them are there?"

"Three or four."

"No, there are six. I saw them!"

"Quick, let's go and wake up the statues!"

Thus the pigeons flew in all directions, and perched on the statues, woke them up by pecking their hands and then warned them of what was happening.

Soon the alarm had reached every part of the city.

All of them were now at the ready, waiting for the signal that the archangel Gabriel would give from the top of St Mark's bell tower, blowing his long golden trumpet.

Chapter twenty

Apart from his two attempts to chase away pigeons, Alvin, as we saw, did his best all evening to show he had become as well-mannered as a dog can be, and after his conversation with Phoebus, the carrier pigeon, he had lain down very quietly under Gea's chair listening to the music of Florian's small orchestra.

Everything would have gone smoothly if the orchestra, at a certain point, hadn't started playing a waltz from *The Merry Widow*.

From the very first notes, Alvin began to get restless, whining and twitching his whiskers. He could stand anything if he really wanted to. He could even sit through a concert of dodecaphonic music, or a rock track like the ones Gea loved, if truly necessary. Anything but *that* particular waltz.

It was Lady Matilda's very favourite piece of music. *The Merry Widow*'s waltz was the piece of music she listened to it at least twice a day, always on the same crackling record, always on the family's old turntable.

It was too much for Alvin. It was pure torture, and it drove him crazy. He tried not to listen. He tried to think of something else. He even covered his ears with his paws.

It was no use.

The notes of the waltz stung his ears and enveloped him, sticking to his fur. He felt as if he were slowly sinking in a river of honey.

Then, suddenly, he remembered Phoebus' tip, just in time, as it happens, because a particularly twisty violin solo was making his moustache stand on end. Slowly, quietly, he stood up and, with his teeth, undid the knot that kept the leash tied around the leg of Gea's chair. He wriggled between Lord Edward's legs and slowly crept towards the orchestra.

The violinist was just in front of him, his *solo* endless and scratchy. Alvin felt he had to stop him.

He gripped the edge of his jacket between his teeth and gave it a rough tug.

A terrifying flat note broke from the violin, making all the glasses and plates tinkle ominously. Even the people who had been talking and not listening to the music jerked upright in their seats.

"Oh no!..." stammered Gea in despair, looking under her chair and realizing that Alvin wasn't there.

"It was Alvin, wasn't it?" asked Matilda with a trembling voice.

"Woe is us!" lamented Edward. "That terrible animal is ruining our holidays!"

Alvin wriggled quickly through the legs of the other players, and repeated the trick on the trombone player, then, quick as a wink, he dealt with the pianist, the clarinettist and the drummer.

After the first moment of astonishment, someone in the audience began to laugh, and since there's nothing more catching than good humour, the laughter spread across the café and from there to everyone in the square.

Then the double-bass player let out a scream: the black and white dog was gnawing away at his strings!

It was the last straw.

Bursting with indignation the musicians got up and tried to catch the dog among the tables and chairs.

"For goodness' sake, Gea!" shouted Lady Matilda. "Catch him before they do! He needs saving!"

Gea jumped up, and so did Gianni. "May I help you?" he asked.

"Yes, of course, thank you," she replied, starting at once to look around.

The musicians and the waiters were intent on punishing the culprit, but Alvin was quicker than them, and got away. The players gave chase, following him between the tables, while everybody stood up to get a better view of what was going on.

All of a sudden Gea pointed to a corner of the square: "There he is!" she said.

"Ssssh, darling, speak quietly!" whispered Matilda. "Don't let the musicians know where Alvin is!"

"I saw him, down there, under the clock tower..." whispered Gea.

Lady Matilda approached her daughter. "Gea, please, I beg you, save our poor Alvin!" Pale and scared, she spoke rapidly. "Save him from those wild men who are hunting him!"

"Calm down, Mum," said Gea. "Gianni and I are going to get that little devil, Don't worry, I've already seen where he went."

"Really?"

"Trust me," said Gea. "In a few minutes we will be back with Alvin on his leash."

Gea introduced Mum, Dad and Gianni to each other, then she and her new friend set out for the clock tower.

They walked normally until they were at a good distance from the café, then, suddenly Gea said "Off we go!" and started running as fast as she could, followed by Gianni.

Meanwhile at Florian's, things had calmed down again. Lord Edward went to speak to the café's director, to say that he was the owner of that dreadful little dog, that he was terribly sorry, and that the dog had run away even though he was on a leash. In conclusion, Lord Edward said that he wanted to pay for the damage.

187

The director smiled graciously. "Thank you for your thoughtfulness, but it was an accident. Don't worry about it."

"Well, we caused no small trouble for the musicians," said Lord Edward, taking his wallet from his pocket. "Please, I want to pay."

"It doesn't matter, believe me..." repeated the director.

Lord Edward took some bills from his wallet and gave them to the man. "These are for the musicians, with my apologies," he said. He didn't need to add "this is an order", yet the employee of Florian's understood the message all the same.

Edward went back to his table, while the musicians prepared their sheet music and tuned up their instruments. As they were about to play again, a powerful trumpet note rang across the square from the top of St Mark's bell tower.

In silence they all looked up. Above them, out of nowhere, all of a sudden, appeared a fantastic sight: a host of flying angels, dragons, winged horses and cherubs. Around them whirled hundreds of pigeons and seagulls, led by Phoebus.

Suddenly, the thunderous galloping of a colossal horse could be heard.

Everybody turned to where the noise was coming from, and saw a great bronze warrior, Colleoni, burst into the square astride his mighty horse. His face was haughty and he grasped his commander's baton in his right hand.

The Moors of the Clock, armed with their long hammers, rode down from their tower on winged horses. They were followed by Justice, St Theodore, St Mark, and the gigantic Archangel Gabriel, golden and gleaming in the evening light.

And then a great and joyful roar echoed round the square, as the Lion of St Mark's, rid at last of his column and his fear of failure, swooped confidently and with great ease around the square.

The only statues that did not free themselves - and that, indeed, seemed to shrink closer together - were the Four Moors.

Everybody, people, animals, statues and birds, moved all together towards a point of the great square, one of the corners of St Mark's Basilica. Soon, angels touched wings with birds, and tourists, dragons, actresses, gondoliers, musicians, cherubs, horses, autograph hounds and paparazzi. Even Cato the cat and his faithful fellows turned up, curious to see what all the noise was about.

Matilda and Edward, fearing that this was yet another Alvin-made disaster, also fought their way to the centre of the crowd, followed by Gianni's father, the producer and the Texan oilman. In the meantime, someone alerted a group of policemen, who arrived and set up a big spotlight on a high bracket, pointing the beam at the basilica wall.

Colleoni got off his horse and clawed his way toward the corner of the basilica, giving short, sharp orders to marshal the chaotic horde of men and statues.

"Hey you lazy squids!" he thundered on arriving at the centre of the scene. "What are you doing? What's going on here?"

The statue of Justice stomped up and drew herself to her full height in front of him, a frown on her face as she glared up at him. "How dare you call me a lazy squid?" she shouted. "This is an outrage! I'm Justice!"

Colleoni, astounded, covered his mouth with his gauntleted hand. "By the handle of my most trusty sword!" he exclaimed. "I apologise, Madam, I didn't see you!"

Justice raised her big sword and pointed it at the basilica. "There are three thieves in there, beyond the marble slabs of that wall!"

"By Mars!" exclaimed Colleoni. "And how the devil did they get into that wall?"

"I saw them, "replied Justice. "They pushed the wall here and there and opened a passage. I don't know how they did it, but I know for sure that they are inside!"

"Well, let's flush them out!" said Colleoni. He crouched near the wall and slammed his great bronze fist into it repeatedly. "Hey, you crooks," he cried with his deep, rusty voice. "Get out of there!"

A deep silence followed the sound of his words. Then the crowd heard noises coming from beyond the wall. Moments went by, then a distant and barely perceptible voice was heard by the crowd. "Here I am, I'm coming..." said the voice.

One of the slabs began to move, then, slowly, it opened to the left. A second slab opened turning to the right. Finally a face appeared. Volauvent's face.

"Please, get me out of here!," said the face.

Two policemen pulled him out.

"Where are the other two?" demanded Justice.

"They're coming," said Volauvent, dusting himself off. After a while another face appeared, Rubino's.

"And what about the third?" asked Justice, in an imperious tone.

"I think he's going to have trouble getting out," said Volauvent. "He's a little large."

A couple of minutes went by but nobody arrived. A policeman shone a torch along the narrow passage. "I can't see anyone's face," he said. "I see just a couple of shoes."

"But are they moving?" asked Justice, impatiently.

190

"Yes, the shoes are coming a little at a time," said the policeman.

Indeed, after another minute, the shoes, hopping like two penguins, were seen at the entrance of the passage.

"Get him out!" ordered Colleoni.

Two big angels grabbed one leg each and pulling hard, they forced poor Muscleton to come out.

"And the stolen goods?" cried Justice. "Where are the stolen goods?"

"What stolen goods, Your Grace?" asked Volauvent, polite as can be, with an expression on his face worthy of the most innocent choirboy. "We didn't steal anything!"

"Don't lie, otherwise I will turn you into statues!" said Justice.

"Your Grace..."

"Don't call me Your Grace!" shouted the statue with her powerful voice "I'm Justice!"

"I apologise, Ms Justice: we aren't thieves. I'm an archaeologist," announced Volauvent with a solemn voice, "and these two men are my assistants. We made an important discovery that will enrich your museum's collection to no end. We found..." he said, drawing out his words, and pausing for a moment to increase the suspense, "we found... a secret room with lots of gold pieces!"

"I don't believe you," insisted Justice. "Search these crooks!"

The policemen searched them thoroughly, but nothing was found in any of their pockets.

Colleoni ordered the policemen into the tunnel to make a careful inspection of the gold room. Two men went into the hole and came back after ten minutes.

"We have proof that nothing is missing," said one of them. "Everything is covered with dust, no one has touched any of the pieces."

Justice was incredulous. "But are you sure no piece has been stolen?"

"Yes, because if anything were missing, we would be able to see it," said the policeman.

"Tell me: how can you see something that's missing?" asked Colleoni, pointing his baton at the policeman.

"If something were missing, Sir, it would have left a spot without dust. As there isn't any dustless spot anywhere on the table, we can safely assume that nothing has been stolen."

Colleoni gazed for a long time at the three men. "Hmm... I'm not convinced," he said.

"Neither am I," said Justice. "But how can we put them in jail without a charge?"

In the meantime the chief of the police and the mayor, amidst a group of policemen, had reached the centre of the great crowd that had gathered around the corner of St Marks's Basilica .

"What kind of mess is this?" the mayor shouted grumpily. "What are all these statues doing here? Why is the lion of St Mark flying around the square? What does he think he is? A helicopter?"

The two policemen who had inspected the secret room gave their reports to the mayor, specifying that the three men who had discovered the secret room were suspected thieves, even if nothing in the room had been stolen.

"Don't waste time on this riddle," said the mayor. "If you can prove they stole something, throw them in jail, otherwise let them go. And tell the statues to go back to their places."

Just then, Gea and Gianni arrived on the scene. Alvin was with them, firmly kept on his leash by Gianni. They had surprised him in a blind lane, and together they had caught him. And this time they wouldn't have him run away again.

The fox-terrier, as we know, is a dog full of fighting spirits, so, when he saw all those big, strange statues, he thought that they were dangerous monsters to be barked and growled at. In fact, he started barking with all the breath in his lungs.

Right after, St Mark's square echoed with the sound of a deep, angry voice.

"There he is, there he is!" cried the voice. "There's the dog that stole my sausage! Catch him, I want him dead or alive!"

The voice belonged to a man you will certainly remember. He was the huge shopkeeper from whom Alvin had stolen three yards of sausage.

Gea, in two seconds, grasped the problem: that affair of the stolen sausage had to be another mess made by Alvin!

In fact, a big, sweaty and nasty man was running at full speed towards them. "Off we go!" Gea cried. "Run Gianni, run!"

Another desperate voice echoed across the square as Lady Matilda urged her husband into action: "Edward, for goodness' sake, stop them!"

For a couple of seasons, during his student years, Edward had been the proud winner of an intercollege cross-country championship, and although he didn't feel like jumping fences or ditches right now, a short sprint wasn't out of his possibility.

So he started chasing the big man, calling him. After a hundred yards Edward was so close to him that the man finally understood that someone was running after him. The shopkeeper stopped and turned to see who wanted him so urgently.

"What is it?" asked the big man.

"I heard..." said Edward, catching his breath "... I heard you shouting something about sausages and a dog ... a dog dead or alive..."

"Yes, exactly, and sooner or later I'll get that damned beast!" said the shopkeeper angrily.

"Could you describe the dog you are after?"

"Sure. He is a little black and white pest with whiskers, a beard and..."

"He's my dog," interrupted Edward, with a smile.

The man lost his temper. "So what your dog has done isn't enough for you!" he shouted, raising a hand more or less as large as a frying pan, and trying to grab Edward with it. "And now you're pulling my leg as well!"

Edward shielded himself. "No, no, calm down!" he cried. "I didn't mean to make fun of you, I just want to pay the damage done by my dog!"

The shopkeeper dropped his hand to his side and stared incredulous at Edward. "I did hear you right? You're really saying that you want to *pay* me?"

"Yes, of course," said Edward, taking the wallet out of his jacket.

"Unbelievable..." said the big man, scratching his head. "This is the first time in my life that I've been chased by someone who wants to pay me!"

Lord Edward paid his debt, then, as soon as the shopkeeper left, called Gea on her phone.

"Where are you, darling?" he asked.

"Oh, at least one mile away from that big gorilla," replied Gea. "He wanted to kill Alvin!"

"No, don't worry, Gea, I took care of everything, he's not chasing you anymore," said Edward. "Poor fellow, he's got a point. Alvin stole three yards of sausage from his shop. Did you catch the little devil?"

"Yes, he's on his leash, and I swear he won't get away again!"

"All right, we'll wait for you at Florian's."

Chapter twenty-one

While all of this was going on, the crowd that had gathered at the basilica corner had begun to thin out.

The first to fly away were the winged statues, the saints, angels, cherubs, horses and dragons. Then Colleoni got back on his horse, the statue of Justice climbed back onto her pedestal, the Lion of St Mark's settled once again on top of his column with Phoebus and his friends perched on his wings, Cato and his feline gang returned to the Rialto Market. The paparazzi turned off their cameras, the autograph hunters closed their notepads. The city dwellers, the tourists, and Tony and his fellow gondoliers all went away.

Gianni's father and his friends from the Lido Film Festival, not yet ready to call it a night, remained in the square, taking their places again at Florian's.

And Volauvent, Rubino and Muscleton? What happened to them?

As soon as the police chief dismissed them with a wave of his hands, they made off as fast as they could, and only when they were far enough from St Mark's square did they allow themselves to sit down on the steps of a bridge.

"You owe me your life," panted Volauvent. "You do know it, don't you?"

"Yes, we do," replied Rubino.

"You were right," admitted Muscleton. "That gold was untouchable. If we'd come out of there with two sacks of gold, we'd have been in jail right now. Or turned into statues."

"And even if we hadn't, half of Venice would have been waiting for us outside," added Volauvent, "we would have had cops all over us wherever we went. That treasure was too much for us."

Just then, they saw a little girl coming towards them with a very young boy who was holding a little black and white dog on a leash. They were strolling slowly, and chatting pleasantly,

"Hey, see those two?" whispered Rubino. "She's the Peacoks' daughter..."

Gea and Gianni reached the bridge and began to climb the ladder. As they passed the three men, Alvin stopped, all four paws firmly on the ground, straining against the onward pull of the leash. He sniffed the air and stared at the figures beside him. "Here they are again, those ugly brutes," he thought.

Gea and Gianni, too, recognised the three crooks that had come out of the hole in the basilica wall.

Alvin wrinkled his nose, bared his teeth at them, and started growling. Frightened, the three men stood up and drew back. Rubino tried to kick him, but Alvin dodged out the blow, and if Gianni had not held a firm grip on his leash, he'd certainly have bitten the thief's leg. After which, the dog barked at them so loudly that his voice echoed among the houses. The three men, at that point, cut and ran.

Gea bent down to pet and praise her dog. "Yes Alvin, you're really a nice, brave dog," she said, stroking him, "but now do be quiet, otherwise someone's going to pour a bucket of water on us."

"But why was he so angry with those men?" asked Gianni.

"Yes, Alvin, tell us why you were so mad at those men," whispered Gea. "But please," she added, "keep your barking down..."

Alvin, barking as softly as he could, told her that the three chased him off the Rialto bridge and through the glass factory, breaking everything in an attempt to catch him...

"Oh, that's terrible!" said Gea.

"What's going on?" asked Gianni.

"Alvin said that those three bad guys tried to catch him!" replied Gea, frightened.

Gianni gazed at Gea and her dog with eyes wide with amazement.

"But... are you saying that you understand Alvin's barking?"

"Yes, of course," replied Gea, as if this were the most natural thing in the world.

"Incredible," said Gianni, looking at Gea with admiration. "How did you learn to do that?"

"Simple. I think that if you really believe in something, odds are that it will come true."

"Can you speak with other animals?", he asked.

"Sure. Besides dogs, I learned to speak with cats, parrots and monkeys," said Gea. "Now, I'm trying to learn to speak with the geese belonging to our neighbours in the countryside, but they are really annoying; they are gossipy and overbearing, and they quarrel with other animals, and also with kids, as a matter of fact."

"As for me, when I was a child, my parents gave me a hamster," said Gianni. "I tried to speak with him, but it was useless."

"I tried to speak with a hamster too," said Gea, "but besides «I'm hungry», «I'm sleepy» and «I've got a tummy ache», I didn't manage to get anything else from him."

"Maybe hamsters are a bit stupid."

"I think so. Once I tried to read a poem by Lord Byron to him. The only thing he managed to say was «I'm sleepy». I tried a second time with something easier, *If*, by Rudyard Kipling. Can you guess what my hamster's reply was?"

"No," said Gianni.

"He replied «I've got a tummy ache»," said Gea. "Poor little things, hamsters are hopeless."

"Perhaps that is the reason why kids love little animals," said Gianni. "When my hamster looked at me, it felt as if he were saying "Please don't leave me alone, protect me...""

"Yes, I think so too," agreed Gea. "Now we'd better go, Gianni. Our parents are waiting for us."

But what happened to the three thieves after they got away from the bridge where the little dog tried to bite Rubino's leg?

After a few minutes of silent walking, Volauvent, Rubino and Muscleton stopped at another bridge.

"Listen, friends, we have a decision to make," said Volauvent. "We've had some close calls in all our years together, but nothing compares with this evening. Dicey, dicey it was, and I'm sick of it all!"

"Sick of all what?" asked Muscleton.

"After what we went through tonight my only wish is to forget the whole business."

"The whole business? Are you kidding us?" asked Rubino, astonished.

"Not at all. I don't want to spend the rest of my days in prison," replied Volauvent. "We spent a lot of time running after a family on a wild goose chase. And as if that wasn't enough, we had to be attacked by their dog! Ah, that was really the last blow for me! Let me tell you the bitter truth: we are third-rate thieves!"

"But we scored big loads of times!" protested Muscleton.

Volauvent smiled, but it was a bitter smile. "Big loads of times?" he asked. "Come on, Muscleton, let's not blow things out of proportion," said Volauvent. "Anyhow, times have changed."

"But what else could we do now?" asked Muscleton.

"I think that each of us should make his own choices. As far as I'm concerned, I have a confession to make. When I told the police chief that I was an archaeologist, I wasn't kidding him."

"What?" asked Rubino, surprised.

"I know that it's hard for you to take me seriously, but I do have an archaeology degree from the Sorbonne."

"Are you serious?" asked Muscleton.

"Yes, and that's what I'm going to do. I'm going to look for a job as an archaeologist!"

"But... what about Muscleton and me?" asked Rubino.

"I could be a gondolier," said Muscleton. "I love rowing a gondola."

"Do you remember the million in damages that we owe to a certain Murano glassmaker?" asked Rubino.

"I'll grow a long beard. You could be a gondolier, too," replied Muscleton, smiling.

"No, too much water in Venice," said Rubino. "I'm not a fish..."

"So, what would you like to do?" asked Volauvent.

"Let's wait and see..." muttered Rubino.

So it was that the three thieves went their separate ways.

When Gea, Gianni and Alvin got to St Mark's square, Florian's was closed, but the chairs and tables were still there. So were Lady Matilda, Lord Edward, Gianni's father and Mr Webster, chatting pleasantly about the Venice Film Festival and the film directed by Gianni's father, and produced by Mr Webster.

When Gea and Gianni joined them, Lady Matilda took Alvin, cuddling and smothering him with passionate kisses.

Meanwhile, Gea told them how they met by chance the three crooks that had come out of the hole in the basilica's corner, and how Alvin had scared them off.

Gianni reported his extraordinary encounter with Neptune, and the fantastic tales that the sea god told him.

Gianni's father invited Lady and Lord Peacock to his film *première* at the Festival the following week.

And they all agreed how incredibly beautiful the city was, especially at night, when it was silent, and a full moon was shining, as it was that summer night.

Gianni bent toward Gea's ear. "How long will you stay in Venice?" he whispered.

"Another five days, I believe."

"My father will be very busy, next week," said Gianni. "Do you think I could spend some time with you and your parents?"

"Oh, that would be great!" answered Gea.

She asked her parents, and Gianni asked his father. They all agreed.

"You do know that we still have a lot of things to see in Venice, don't you?" said Edward. "Well, I'll tell you what I would like to do. First, another vaporetto ride along the Grand Canal, then a visit to St Mark's Basilica, the Doge's Palace, and the wonderful Accademia Gallery."

Everybody approved. Even Gianni's father said that he would be glad to join them, schedule permitting.

"There is another thing I'd love to do," Lord Edward added. "I'd like to stroll peacefully along the streets, up and down the bridges."

"On one condition," said Lady Matilda, with a voice that pretended to be stern. "That-Alvin-doesn't-make-off-again!"

"I solemnly promise that we'll keep a tight hold on him," said Gea. "And if by pure chance he should escape, Gianni and I will catch him straightaway."

"How would you like to see the sunrise?" asked Gianni's father.

His suggestion was willingly accepted by the Peacocks, and of course by Gianni, as well. They crossed the square, went by the Doge's Palace and under the column on top of which stood the winged Lion. Then they stopped short of the edge of the quay overlooking the sea.

The moon, after its long night voyage across the sky of Venice, finally set. For a short while, the sky turned dark again, and the stars reappeared, but a light rose colour spread out in the sky, announcing the rise of the sun.

They all stood in silence, enchanted by the marvellous sight of that daybreak.

Suddenly they heard a noise under the quay, as if something were splashing in the seawater.

Gianni bent down, and immediately pointed to the water.

"Look, look over there!" he shouted, "it's a dolphin... Oooh, but it's Silverskin! My friend Silverskin!"

All of them saw that actually there was a dolphin under the quay, his head peeping out of the water, a cheerful and confident expression on his face. Gianni got down on his knees and stretched out his arm towards the dolphin, offering his hand to him.

"Come on, Silverskin, let me touch you!" said Gianni.

The dolphin, slowly, lifted his body out of the water, higher and higher, until it seemed he could magically stay standing on the sea surface. Silverskin saw Gianni's outstretched hand, and with a last effort, with a final wriggle, he managed to reach the palm of his hand, pressing it gently, for just a moment, with the point of his muzzle.

After that, the dolphin slid down into the water, keeping his head out, then he sang a mysterious, cracking and whistling song. to Gianni.

Gianni, smiling, turned towards Gea. She smiled too. He was amazed.

"Gea, it's incredible…" he said, beaming. "I understood what the dolphin said to me!"

"Me too," said Gea. "I'm so happy…"

But enchantments never last more than a moment. Silverskin performed a joyous pirouette, dived into the water and disappeared.

41629513R00114

Printed in Poland
by Amazon Fulfillment
Poland Sp. z o.o., Wrocław